Quietly, Seth went on. ''Jet, I had no right to attack your character.''

''Are—are you also sorry you kissed me?'' Jet wondered why her palms were suddenly damp.

Seth stared at her and she saw various shades of feeling cross his face. Finally he replied, ''No, I don't believe I am.'' He hesitated. ''Jet, you and I—it's been—an experience. A remarkably stimulating experience at times,'' he added with a brief attempt at humor.

His next words caused a dull ache in Jet.

''But I'm committed to Marian, as you so rightly pointed out. She suits me. And she'll have good reason to be angry if I find you yet another job. So I'm afraid you're on your own, butterfly....

Kay Gregory is married, lives in Canada and has two grown-up sons. She recently began writing for Harlequin, and readers will welcome her latest novel in the Harlequin line.

Books by Kay Gregory

HARLEQUIN ROMANCE
2919—A STAR FOR A RING
3016—A PERFECT BEAST

Impulsive Butterfly

Kay Gregory

Harlequin Books

TORONTO • NEW YORK • LONDON
AMSTERDAM • PARIS • SYDNEY • HAMBURG
STOCKHOLM • ATHENS • TOKYO • MILAN

Original hardcover edition published in 1989
by Mills & Boon Limited

ISBN 0-373-03058-4

Harlequin Romance first edition June 1990

This book is dedicated to
my mother-in-law, Joan Gregory
And in memory of
my father-in-law, Sid Gregory
with love and gratitude.

CHAPTER ONE

'WHAT an extraordinarily beautiful girl,' murmured Seth.

He thought he was talking to himself, but Marian, who rarely missed anything whether she was meant to hear it or not, moved immediately around her desk and came to stand beside him at the window.

'Where?' she asked sharply, the habitual reserve surprisingly absent from her voice.

Seth glanced at her speculatively and gestured across the busy Vancouver street. 'Over there. By the jeweller's.'

'There are *three* jewellers "over there",' replied Marian tartly.

Seth drew a quick breath and his brown eyes narrowed slightly as he glanced again at the trim blonde secretary who had recently become his fiancée. He remembered it was her literal, no-nonsense approach to life that had attracted him to her in the first place—so he nodded.

'Right. I meant the jeweller on the corner.' His warm baritone had a faintly malicious ring to it as he added, 'With the beautiful girl in front of it staring up at this office.'

'Oh. You mean the one in the flowered skirt who looks like a gypsy. All that untidy black hair...'

'Very dark brown really,' Seth contradicted her. And then, surprising himself as much as Marian, he announced, 'I think it's very attractive.'

He did, too. In a gesture of uncharacteristic care-
lessness, he ran a large hand through his own thick
burnished hair and studied the girl more closely.
Long, waving dark locks, wide brown eyes that
slanted up at the corners, a warm, generous
mouth—and the most perfectly shaped oval face he
had seen outside the movies. Even her complexion
was golden and glowing with life. He turned his
head a fraction to get a better angle—and caught
sight of Marian's cool blue eyes fixed on him with
obvious disapproval.

Mentally shaking himself, Seth tore his gaze away
from the vision in the red flowered skirt and smiled
tightly at his fiancée. She was right, of course. The
girl across the street was definitely not his type.
Pushing his hands into the pockets of well-cut, dark
blue trousers, he swung back into his office and
slammed the door shut behind him.

Because he was no longer watching her, Seth
didn't see the subject of his attention take a long,
deep breath, hoist her red bag firmly across her
shoulder and step purposefully into the street.

A few moments later, on the landing outside the
office, Jet Kellaway paused, patted at her long hair
in a futile attempt to control it, and with another
determined breath stepped on to the grey plush
carpet of the Hagan Employment Agency.

At the back of the large, airy room two young
and very attractive women looked up from their
computer terminals to cast quick, appraising glances
at the newcomer. In front of them sat a middle-
aged, bespectacled receptionist who smiled at Jet,
asked her business, then murmured into an in-
tercom. A few minutes later she was told Miss
Sinclair would see her in her office.

As Jet pushed open the door, Marian looked up slowly from the job specification she was studying, and raised her carefully plucked eyebrows.

'Yes?' she said coldly, in a voice that would have crushed a less optimistic person than Jet Kellaway, who instead of being crushed smiled cheerfully and said she had come about a job.

'So I had imagined,' replied Marian repressively.

Jet wasn't repressed. 'Yes. So if I could fill out an application form, or whatever it is you do here...'

'What *we* do here, Miss...?'

'Kellaway. Jet Kellaway.'

Marian tightened her lips and continued, 'What *we* do here, Miss Kellaway, is place suitable people in the positions we are asked to fill. What *you* do is convince us you're suitable.'

Jet's shoulders sagged a little. 'You don't think I am, do you?' she sighed.

'I've no idea,' Marian's voice cracked back at her. 'You haven't yet told me what you do.'

'Mostly I change jobs,' replied Jet, with more honesty than self-interest.

Marian closed her eyes. Behind her, Jet noticed a solid oak door open slightly as a man's hand appeared in the crack. A nice hand, she noted approvingly. Big, with strong, square-tipped fingers and blunt, very clean-looking nails. Not a labourer's hand, but one that was surely capable of accomplishing whatever it set out to do...

'Miss Kellaway!' The woman behind the desk was glaring at her, and Jet realised she had been daydreaming—again—and that all hopes of a job with the Hagan Agency were rapidly slipping away.

'Sorry,' she murmured guiltily, 'I didn't quite catch what you said.'

'I *asked*,' almost shouted Marian, 'whether you had any particular job you usually change.'

As soon as she spoke the door behind her swung open and the owner of the hand stepped quickly into the room.

'That'll do, Marian,' snapped Seth, in a voice which sent shivers up Jet's spine. 'There's no need to shout at our applicants. If you're feeling a little tired, why don't you get yourself a cup of coffee? I'll see to Miss Kellaway myself.'

Marian's mouth opened, closed again, and then without replying she shot Jet a look of loathing, swung open her door and disappeared from view. Jet could hear her black heels snapping sharply against the parquet. She glanced curiously up at the man who had rescued her from what had promised to be a thoroughly disastrous interview.

Mm. Nice. A little rigid, perhaps, but on the whole the rest of him matched the hand. Not exceptionally tall, just under six feet at a guess, but well-built. Good shoulders, firm thighs atop nice solid legs, a strong neck—and oh, *yes*, a definitely—arresting—face. It wasn't handsome, exactly. Too unusual, with the prominent cheekbones, wide-set, clear, almost dangerously gentle brown eyes and those utterly incredible lips above the slightly cleft chin. It was the lips that made her stare. They weren't wide, but just right, curved in a way she had always thought men's lips should not be, full, indescribably sensuous—and yet sensitive somehow...

With an effort of will she forced her eyes upwards, noted the broad forehead and thick, shining brown hair—cut rather too short, she decided—and realised he was waving her into his office. Just before he turned away she caught him studying her with a curious, appraising look which made her wonder if he knew she had been admiring him. Yes, of course he did. He was probably used to being admired. Expected it, in fact. And, come to think of it, he was just the sort of man she normally avoided like the plague. In her experience that type was always conceited, self-satisfied, and convinced they could have whatever—or whoever—they wanted with one lordly snap of the fingers. Gino had been like that. Only then she had been too young and naïve to recognise the pattern.

'Sit down, Miss Kellaway.'

At least someone in this office was finally going to offer her a seat. Jet sank down thankfully and saw him reach for a cigarette from a silver case on the desk, then change his mind and lean back in his chair. The fabric of his white shirt stretched enticingly across his impressive chest. Jet swallowed and waited for him to speak. When he didn't, but continued to study her thoughtfully, with his fingers strumming absently on his desk, she took the bull by the horns and told him she'd come about a job.

'So I gathered.'

Oh, lord, did everyone around here take that supercilious tone?

'What sort of a job?' he asked finally, in a voice which Jet noticed for the first time was warm, deep and, for such a controlled, serious-looking man, quite remarkably sexy.

She smiled hopefully. 'Any sort of job, Mr...?'

'Hagan. Seth Hagan.'

'Oh. Oh, I see. You're the head honcho around here, then?'

Seth's eyebrows lifted slightly. 'I suppose you could put it that way.'

'But I shouldn't have?'

He sighed. 'You can put it any way you like, Miss Kellaway. And yes, I do own this agency. Or have done since my father retired.'

'Oh, it's a family business, then?'

'It is. Do you always ask all the questions at your interviews?' There was a small smile on the lips she was trying so hard to keep her mind off, but she heard the edge to his voice.

'No. I'm sorry,' she said quickly. 'I just meant...'

'Never mind.' He leaned towards her, his elbows on the desk and his square-tipped fingers touching as he asked levelly, 'Is it clerical work you're looking for, Miss Kellaway?'

'No, not really. I can't type.'

'All right, what can you do?'

'Oh, almost anything...'

'Bookkeeping, data entry, switchboard...?'

'No. No, I don't do office work. Although I wouldn't mind trying.'

Seth closed his eyes. 'I bet you wouldn't. What *are* you best at, Miss Kellaway? Apart from changing jobs?'

'Well, I don't know.' She glanced at him quickly, almost anxiously. 'I've looked after children, worked in stores and lots of fast-food outlets. I've been a waitress, I worked for a dry cleaner and a pizza factory, a health-food bar and—I've done some soliciting...'

'Whoa! Hold it.' Seth held up a hand, his expression suddenly wary. 'Soliciting *what*?' he asked slowly.

'Not what you think,' replied Jet indignantly. Her wide mouth turned down in a grimace of self-derision. 'As a matter of fact, I was selling cemetery plots—until the day a charming elderly lady answered the phone and told me she would be in her grave soon enough, thank you, without any encouragement from me. I felt she had a point.'

'So you quit.'

Just for a moment Jet thought she saw a gleam of amusement in Seth's eyes, but as he went on she decided she must have made a mistake, because there was nothing remotely amused about the man who fixed her with a look that made her want to hit him, and said coldly, 'Miss Kellaway, this is not an agency for young women who take jobs to amuse themselves when they can find nothing better to do. I'm sorry, but I don't hire butterflies, not even pretty ones, so I really don't think there's much point in your filling out an application. It would be wasting both your time and mine.'

Jet felt bright colour flood her cheeks as she jumped hotly to her feet. 'Oh, well, I wouldn't want to waste *your* valuable time, Mr Hagan,' she jeered, in a voice that dripped with sarcasm. 'I'm sure you're a very busy man—as well as an exceptionally rude one. But just for your information you *did* ask me what I could do, and I am *not* a butterfly, pretty or otherwise. I've never been a bit amused by my jobs—precisely the opposite usually—and I don't work just for something to do. I need to eat, Mr Hagan.' Her voice cracked slightly. 'And I don't want the government to support me, because I'm young enough, healthy enough—and crazy enough too, I suppose, to think I can support myself. I apologise for taking up your time.'

Without looking at him again, she picked up her red bag, turned on her heel, and with her head held high and her dark hair swinging behind her she marched angrily out of his office.

To the wide-eyed interest of two computer operators and a receptionist, Seth caught up with her just as she reached the outer door. When she felt his hand on her arm, she gasped.

'Just a minute, Miss Kellaway.' He hadn't raised his voice, but there was something about it that told Jet there was no question of not waiting. This man expected to be obeyed. And, surprising herself, she stopped immediately and lifted her eyes up to his. Not very far up, she noted. He wasn't a great deal taller than she was, although just at the moment he seemed it.

She drew in her breath. 'Yes, Mr Hagan?' Her voice was deliberately bored.

For a moment he said nothing as his eyes roamed quickly over her body—passing judgement, thought Jet indignantly—and came to rest on her face.

'If I was rude, I apologise,' he said finally. A flicker of a smile crossed his lips. 'But you must admit you have a very odd way of going about getting a job.'

'Have I? Well, you have a very odd way of treating your applicants. For a start, you can take your hand off my arm.'

Seth glanced down at the hand curled a little too tightly near her elbow—and let her go as if he thought the contact would burn him. Which wasn't likely, she thought. But, noting with a start the warm feeling on her arm and the sense of something missing when he released her, she wondered for a moment if perhaps he might have singed her. Then she shook her head, dismissing such nonsense, and said firmly, 'Mr Hagan, as you have already told me you don't have a job for me, perhaps we can stop wasting *my* time.'

'Mm. I suppose that's a dose of my own medicine.' He brushed his hand over his mouth, and for the first time Jet thought she saw appreciation in his eyes.

She smiled faintly. 'I suppose it is.'

'Hmm.' He stared at her, his gaze impenetrable, giving nothing away. Then he nodded slightly, appearing to make up his mind.

'I was wrong. Maybe I do have a job for you. Besides, you're much too thin.'

Jet gasped at him. 'And *what*,' she said, after a brief silence, during which she was irritated to hear the receptionist stifle a giggle, 'has my figure got to do with a job?'

Seth put his hand up to his forehead, covering wryly bewildered eyes that for a moment seemed to have changed from brown to green. 'Damned if I know,' he admitted. He smiled disarmingly. 'Come back into my office a moment, Miss Kellaway. Perhaps we can figure it out.'

Jet opened her mouth to tell him to go to hell, heard a snicker from one of the young women, and found herself following him instead. She observed, to her chagrin, that he had precisely the sort of back she liked to follow. Trousers fitting nicely around the hips and thighs, a sexy, swinging gait, and shoulders not rigid, but just casually stooped.

Funny that, because her first impression of Seth Hagan had been of a taut, unbending Monument to Control.

Once more he was waving her to a chair as he lowered himself behind his neatly ordered desk.

Jet decided she had better take charge of this situation before it took charge of her. 'Mr Hagan,' she said quietly, 'so far since I came into this office your secretary has shouted at me, you have told me that I'm wasting your time because I don't really need a job—and now you're making remarks about my figure. On the whole, I think I've just about had enough.'

To Jet's amazement, Seth grinned, and it changed his face so completely that she nearly fell off her chair. In repose it was an attractive, arresting but serious sort of face. Then, when his lips parted in that wide, irresistible and unconsciously sexy grin, his attraction was so immediate, so physical and alive, that Jet wanted to reach out a hand to touch him. Just for a moment she thought she saw her feelings reflected in his eyes, too. Then the grin faded, and his face was impassive again as he said equably, 'I don't blame you, Miss Kellaway. The truth is, I've never had anyone like you apply for a job before. I'm afraid you took me by surprise.'

'Surprise?'

'Mm. Most people come in here wearing neat dark suits with their hair sleekly combed or tied back, and they give my secretary their best business smiles and tell her they have a wonderfully steady work record, but for reasons beyond their control they just happen to need a new job. You, on the other hand, breeze in looking like spring in a red flowered skirt, with that marvellous hair flowing down your back—and inform my very organised secretary that "mostly you change jobs".'

'You heard me?' asked Jet, annoyed with herself because she was pleased he liked her hair.

'I did. These walls weren't built for privacy, I'm afraid. And I knew it was you the moment I heard your voice.'

Jet stared at him. He didn't look so formidable any more, and there was something very appealing about his eyes. 'What on earth are you talking about?' she asked resignedly.

'You. I saw you standing across the street. And when I heard you speak to Marian, I guessed at once it was you.'

Jet eyed him doubtfully. He was reaching for a cigarette again, and this time he placed the filter tip between his lips and lit it. Smoke curled up from his nostrils as he leaned back and inhaled.

'I don't see how you *could* know it was me,' she said finally. Then she smiled. 'But as a matter of fact I saw you at the window. That's why I came in here first instead of to the agency next door. I thought if you had time to stand at the window and stare, your company might be more relaxed and comfortable to deal with.' She sighed. 'But I was wrong, wasn't I?'

'Were you?'

'Well, wasn't I?' Jet stirred restlessly and crossed one long leg over the other. 'Mr Hagan, before I leave, please satisfy my curiosity about one thing. What *has* my figure got to do with finding a job? What I mean is—what kind of an agency is this? And what kind of a job do you really have in mind? It's obviously not clerical.' Her voice held an undertone of indignant accusation.

Seth's full lips turned down slightly and she saw
muscles move convulsively in his throat. The
expression in his wide brown eyes was a study in
not altogether amused astonishment.

'Miss Kellaway,' he said repressively, 'I have no
idea what you're thinking, and I really don't want
to know. But to answer your question, this is a
general employment agency. We supply people for
whatever jobs clients have in mind...'

As Jet's lips opened to frame another question,
he added hastily, 'Within the bounds of decency
and the law. And your figure, of course, has
nothing to do with anything.' He took a long drag
on his cigarette and butted it quickly in a large
executive ashtray. 'I meant you looked hungry,
that's all.' He smiled thinly. 'And therefore in need
of a job.'

'Oh.' Jet was not at all sure why his apparent
sympathy made her angry, but she knew quite
definitely that the last thing she wanted from this
superior, judgemental man was pity. With a speed
that made him lift his eyebrows, she jumped
furiously to her feet.

'I'm not a charity case, Mr Hagan. Thank you
for your time.' Without looking at him again, she
turned around and marched towards the door.

Then for the second time that day she felt his
strong hand on her arm. Only this time his grip was
unmistakably too tight, and he was standing very
close because she could feel his hard frame pressed
against her back. To her total surprise, she found
she liked him there. She liked it even more when a
moment later he spun her round to face him and,
with both hands on her shoulders, stood staring into

her face. He really was extraordinarily attractive—
all glowering and physical like that.

'Please don't throw tantrums in my office, Miss
Kellaway. It doesn't impress me at all.'

Jet stopped liking him near her, and wished she
could send him to Mars. Preferably in a self-
destructing shuttle.

'Take your hands off me, Mr Hagan.' Each word
was separate and clipped short.

Again that look of confusion passed briefly over
Seth's face. But he removed his hands and stepped
quickly away from her.

'I'm sorry,' he said curtly. 'Very unprofessional
of me. Miss Kellaway—can you dust and sweep
floors?'

His words were so unexpected that Jet felt her
anger evaporate and turn into a totally unexpected
urge to laugh.

'Are you crazy?' she asked, giving in to the urge
without a struggle. 'One minute you're playing
Lord of the Concrete Jungle so that I expect to see
you start swinging from the light up there, and the
next you're asking a perfectly healthy woman if she
can *dust*.'

'I think I must be crazy.' Seth shook his head
and lifted his hand to his hair.

'You look much nicer with it all ruffled like that,'
she remarked inconsequentially. 'Not nearly so
starched and pressed.'

Seth glared at her, then he shook his head again
as his lips broke into a slightly bemused smile.

'You're impossible, aren't you?' he managed finally. 'As I said before, *not* my usual style of ap-
plicant at all. But I asked if you could dust because
an office cleaning company we're associated with

has asked us to supply someone for the Sayers-
Tomson building. If you can't type, I'm afraid
that's all we have at the moment. Are you
interested?'

'Oh, yes.' Jet nodded. 'Beggars can't be choosers.
But—that's a huge building, isn't it? It would take
a week to clean.'

Seth sighed. 'Don't be more of an idiot than you
can help, Miss Kellaway. A large staff cleans the
building every night. Joe Mellor is my supervisor
there, and he's just lost one of his girls.'

'Careless of him,' Jet giggled.

'Miss Kellaway...'

'OK. I'm sorry. No levity.' She pursed her wide
mouth primly. 'I'll take your job, Mr Hagan. That
is—if you're offering it to me.'

'Oh, I'm offering it to you, Miss Kellaway. And
no doubt I'm out of my mind.'

'No doubt.' Jet was still looking prim. 'When do
I start?'

'Tonight at six. Here.' He strode back to his desk
and scrawled an address on a piece of paper. 'Ask
for Mr Mellor. He'll tell you what to do.'

'Thank you.' Jet took the proffered paper and
was suddenly and surprisingly shy. Seth Hagan too
appeared unusually tongue-tied as he walked past
her to open the door.

When she reached him he smiled, a warm,
stomach-turning smile, and asked out of the blue,
'What's that scent you're wearing, Miss Kellaway?
I don't think I've encountered it before.'

No, thought Jet a little waspishly, and I'll bet
you've encountered plenty of lures in your time—
all of them applied with the express intention of
baiting the trap for Seth Hagan. Briefly she won-

dered if he had ever been caught—and if he was worth the bait.

But she hid her thoughts and returned his smile easily as she pulled a face and replied with candid unconcern, 'Eau de Herring, I expect, Mr Hagan. I did have a bath before I came, but fish is depressingly persistent.'

CHAPTER TWO

SETH shut his eyes for a moment, but otherwise gave no indication that he found her reply in any way unusual.

'I imagine it can be,' he said drily. Then, determinedly banishing a vision of Jet all soft and wet in a bath, he added, 'As a matter of fact though, I was referring to a much sweeter odour than herring. Something fresh and clean and fragrant. Incidentally—I suppose you wouldn't care to explain what you're talking about?'

Jet didn't think she would much, but could see no quick way out. 'I finished night shift at the fish cannery this morning,' she enlightened him, 'and I just couldn't stand it any more.'

Seth's expression was carefully blank as he studied her face consideringly, trying to read there more than she had said. Then he glanced at his watch and said softly, 'It's twelve o'clock now, Miss Kellaway. Does that mean you haven't had any sleep?'

It was not the reply Jet had expected. 'No,' she admitted quickly, 'I haven't. But I'll get some before this evening so I'll be all right on the job. You'll see.'

'I most certainly won't see,' he informed her. 'I have plans for tonight which I can assure you don't include the Sayers-Tomson building. However, Mr Mellor will see.' He shook his head, as if trying to clear away something which disturbed him, and added irrelevantly, 'What did you do at the fish cannery that you couldn't stand any more?'

Jet sighed. 'You really want to know? I stood at a long trough thing all day taking the roe out of herring. Thousands and thousands of very dead, very smelly herrings that just kept coming and coming. They ship the roe to Japan, you know. We wore rubber boots and gloves, of course, but our feet and hands froze anyway.' She sighed again. 'Some of the women don't mind it because the season is short, the pay is good and they can stand there mentally refurnishing their houses with all the money they're making.'

'But you couldn't do that?'

Jet shook her head. 'I don't have a house to furnish and my small apartment doesn't look any more attractive sprinkled with the fish scales that always fall off my clothes. So I thought if I could find something else to do . . .' She hesitated, noting the grim look on Seth's face, then went on rapidly, 'The herring season is almost over now anyway, so nobody really minds my leaving.'

'I see,' said Seth, remembering that he didn't approve of people who wouldn't stick to their jobs. But the thought of this beautiful girl in rubber gloves and boots gutting dead herring for hours on end just didn't seem to make sense. To his own amazement, he found himself applauding her resignation.

'A wise decision, I expect,' he said equably. Then another, less welcome, idea occurred to him. 'You're going to quit this job for Hagan's too, aren't you?'

Jet looked him straight in the eye. 'I don't expect to make a career of the Sayers-Tomson building,

Mr Hagan. But no, I won't quit without notice and I'll certainly give it my best. I do appreciate your kindness.' She smiled ruefully. 'Especially after the bad start we got off to.'

He nodded. 'Good. I'm glad to hear it.' He held out his hand. Jet took it, and then pulled away with an embarrassed laugh as their feet scuffing on the carpet created an electric current between them.

Seth's eyes followed the red flowered skirt as it disappeared through the door. Then he swung back into his office and was already lighting a cigarette before he sat down at his desk.

He pulled a pad of paper towards him and started to make notes—but found he couldn't concentrate and stared at the light instead. The one that girl—woman?—had said he should be swinging on. Lord of the Concrete Jungle, she had called him. He smiled and shook his head.

It wasn't right, really. With a face like that, Jet Kellaway should be lying on the beach on some tropic isle surrounded by devoted admirers, or dancing the night away in the arms of a hot-blooded, handsome man. A moment later he was irritated, but not altogether surprised, to discover that he was casting himself in the role of that ardent swain. He took another long drag on his cigarette and swore softly under his breath. All the same, it *wasn't* right that Jet should be cleaning that ugly great building. Not that he had had any alternative. There were no jobs on his books she would fit into except that one. And she really did look hungry.

He pulled the pad firmly towards him again, but he had only scrawled a few words when he heard Marian's heels tap into the office next door. He could tell from the way she pulled out her chair and slapped her bag down on her desk that she was still angry. He sighed, rose unhurriedly from his desk and set out to make his peace.

Outside in the hall, Jet touched the handle of the door—and then paused. She had come back to ask whether the job was part-time or full-time, but now she heard a high-pitched feminine voice say shrilly, 'Seth Hagan, you're out of your mind. What's the matter with you today?'

There was a long silence, then she heard Seth reply slowly, 'I'm not at all sure, Marian. But I think you may be right about my mind.'

'Huh,' grunted Marian, reminding Jet forcibly of a mildly disgruntled pig. 'Well, never mind, then, I suppose the damage is done. Where's her application form? I'll give it to Mary to file.'

There was another long silence, followed by Seth's deep voice growling, 'I didn't make her fill one out.'

'What? Seth, stop being ridiculous. Where is it?'

Jet grimaced. Poor Mr Hagan. He certainly had a gorgon for a secretary. She was surprised he put up with it, too. He didn't seem the sort of man to take much nonsense from his staff—or anyone else for that matter. She remembered his words to her about throwing tantrums in his office. From the sound of things, Marian was about to throw one too. She wondered if that authoritative man would take it from the gorgon.

He didn't. 'I told you, I forgot to have one filled out. Now, stop behaving as if I'd committed the crime of the century. Miss Kellaway can do it all tomorrow. Get your coat, Marian, and I'll take you out for lunch.'

'I've already had lunch.'

'A drink, then.'

'I've got work to do. And who's going to run the office?'

'Mary can handle it. Can't you, Mary?'

Someone, presumably the bespectacled receptionist, muttered something Jet couldn't catch. She wondered if Seth Hagan and his secretary always quarrelled in front of the staff.

'You're acting like a silly schoolboy, Seth.' Marian's tone was as sharp and sour as ever. 'Not at all like your sensible self.' She sniffed audibly.

'I'm glad to hear it.' The amusement in his voice was unmistakable now. 'Come on then, my favourite fiancée. Let's end our first—what shall we call it—disagreement?—with a kiss.'

Jet removed her fingers hastily from the handle as it suddenly occurred to her that she had no business to be listening. She could find out about her working hours later.

But as she hurried down the hall she could hear Marian's high voice protesting shrilly that demonstrations of affection were entirely out of place in an office.

Starchy prude, thought Jet, grinning to herself as she stepped into the bright April sunshine. Of course Mr Hagan was a little bit starchy himself, but in a nice sort of way, really. And she was willing to bet her boots he wasn't a prude. No one with lips like his could possibly be a prude. She quickened her pace and glanced at her ancient watch. It was probably wrong as usual, but it was accurate enough to convince her that if she didn't get a move on she would have to get through the first night of her new job on precisely two hours' sleep.

Luckily the first bus that arrived was heading along Fourth Avenue, and half an hour later she was pushing open the door of her poky one-room basement bedsit near to Jericho Beach. Not for the first time, as her eye lit on yet another strip of peeling brown wallpaper, she wished she could save enough money to do some modest redecorating. Or, better still, to move. She sighed, flung her bag on to the floor and slumped down on the divan which also served as her bed.

Through the thin walls she could hear John and Daisy, the students in the equally decaying flat next door, as they banged about making lunch. When the sound of meal preparation stopped abruptly and a spring twanged loudly against the wall, she put up her hands and held them over her ears.

Upstairs, her landlord dropped something heavy and metal with a crash that shook the ceiling as plaster spattered down beside her stove.

Jet groaned. Why *was* it that she never seemed to get ahead, and away from the succession of squalid and run-down rented bedsits? It was seven years now since Gino had left her, and in all that time the longest she had held a job was eight months. She settled a pillow more comfortably behind her head and stared glumly at a damp stain on the ceiling. Of course, she knew part of the answer to her question all too well.

Because she had wanted so much to build a career around teaching children, she had resisted all her relations' efforts to make her take practical subjects at school—things like typing and book-keeping and computers. So that, when she had been

obliged to support herself, she had only been qualified for dull or low-paying jobs. Even so, there
was no reason she couldn't have saved *something*.
At least enough for some kind of teacher training,
if not the degrees in psychology and education she
wanted. But somehow her jobs never seemed to
work out, and what little money she had went on
food and rent and buses.

Jet yawned, and felt her eyes droop. Yes, she
really must get some sleep before she started on this
latest in a long line of dull and dreary jobs. Oh,
well, as she had told that man with the wonderfully
sexy mouth—and the prim and proper fiancée—
beggars couldn't be choosers. And she wasn't quite
a beggar yet. She had told him something of that
sort too, hadn't she? Something about charity...

Her eyelids closed, and the last thing she remembered as she drifted off to sleep was a pair of wide
brown eyes under dark, curving eyebrows—and
full, oh, so full lips above an attractively cleft chin.

Three days later Jet finished cleaning the vice-
president's office and pushed her cart into the
service lift of the Sayers-Tomson building. There
was a faint smile on her lips as she clanged the gates
shut behind her. It really was amazing what you
learned about people when you cleaned up after
them, she mused. The vice-president, for instance,
was obviously an alcoholic, as the daily selection
of empty bottles in his wastepaper basket attested.

She was still smiling when she stepped briskly out
on to the third floor hallway. Then the smile disappeared abruptly as her eye fell on the largest fly
in the ointment of this surprisingly illuminating job.

Joe Mellor, supervising tyrant of the building, was leaning, stopwatch in hand, against the opposite wall. Jet's heart sank into her sandals as she saw the satisfied gleam in his beady little eyes.

'You're thirty seconds late,' he announced with triumphant relish.

'Am I?' asked Jet mildly. And then, her sense of proportion getting the better of her instinct for job preservation, 'Does it matter?'

Joe swelled visibly, and she thought for a moment that his little eyes would pop right out of his face.

'It certainly does,' he almost spat at her. When Jet only stared at him, he shouted unpleasantly, 'And you can wipe that silly grin right off your pretty face. I fail to see what's so amusing.'

Jet sighed, and dutifully wiped the grin. 'As a matter of fact, I was smiling because there are so many interesting things one learns when one cleans offices. I never realised it before.'

Joe glowered at her suspiciously. 'What do you think you're talking about, young lady?'

'People,' explained Jet artlessly. 'You know, bottles in the VP's basket, the betting shop they're running in accounting—and that affair the head of sales is having with his secretary...'

'What?' Joe took a step towards her. 'What on earth are you talking about, girl?'

Oh, dear, thought Jet, now I've done it. He doesn't like me knowing more about the building than he does. 'Hair,' she explained diffidently. 'In his private executive washroom. That and—other things—in strange places.'

Joe's glower became positively venomous. 'Now you listen to me, young woman. You're paid to clean this building, not run a detective agency on the side...'

'But I'm not,' objected Jet. 'I can't work with my eyes closed, Mr Mellor, and how can I help what I see?'

'By getting on with the job, and minding your own business.' His nose began to twitch, which was a sure sign he was enjoying himself. 'I've been timing you with my stopwatch, young woman, and time is money, you know. Waste not want not, many hands make light work...'

'And a stitch in time saves nine,' finished Jet resignedly, anticipating his next well-worn phrase. Joe, halted in mid-quote, gaped at her as she finished quietly, 'Mr Mellor, I really don't work any harder because you happen to have a watch.'

As soon as the words were out of her mouth, she knew that they were fatal. But she had had all she could take of Joe's pettiness and obsession with tired clichés.

Watching his face, she could see self-importance and the desire to retaliate wrestle a winning battle with his own laziness. He didn't really want to dismiss her, because that meant he would be obliged to finish her work himself. On the other hand, the stopwatch with which he timed his staff's return from supper breaks was his favourite symbol of authority, and she had dared to suggest it was trivial.

Shades of indecision flickered in his eyes as his face grew blotched and angry. But in the end, as Jet had known he would, he came down on the side of his dignity and power.

'Fetch your coat, young lady,' he ordered, in a high, spiteful voice. 'Your employment with Hagan's is terminated.'

Pompous creep, thought Jet, pushing her cart towards him so that he had to jump out of the way.

As the gate inched closed behind her she saw the colour slowly leaving Joe's face as he stared disgustedly at the collection of mops and dusters which had just become his responsibility—and she laughed.

She was no longer laughing when, an hour and a half and two buses later, she stumbled wearily into her apartment and noticed that there was yet another damp spot on the wall.

She kicked off her shoes and thumped moodily down in the room's only comfortable chair.

Damn. It had happened again. And this time through no fault of her own. Well—almost no fault of her own. If only Joe Mellor hadn't been such a little dictator.

And if only you could learn to keep your mouth shut, Jet Kellaway, a sober voice murmured inside her head.

Yes—well . . . She picked restlessly at a loose thread in the brown, tweed-covered chair, then shook her head vigorously. It was too much to expect of her. No one but a complete worm would tolerate Joe for long—and a worm was one thing she wasn't. Anyway, in the long run it was all because of that hard-boiled man at the Hagan Employment Agency. He was the one who had hired Joe Mellor in the first place. He probably approved of nit-picking slave-drivers like Joe. No, that wasn't fair. After all, Seth Hagan had been nice enough to employ her when she needed his help.

Gradually Jet's fingers stopped pulling at the hapless thread, and her dark eyes became deep and thoughtful. He had given her one job, hadn't he? Which, whatever Joe said, she had performed quite satisfactorily. And surely even Seth couldn't blame her for Joe's obsession with seconds. Or could he? She remembered the gentle brown eyes which changed colour so easily—and could turn so relentlessly hard. And she wondered.

Well, if nothing else, it was certainly worth trying him again. Besides—she smiled to herself, a little twisted smile—the fact was, she had been thinking about that stiff, but strangely attractive man ever since the day she had met him. And the truth was also that she wanted the opportunity to see him again—just to assure herself that the attraction she had felt was only a figment of her imagination brought on by a case of serious unemployment.

Whatever the reason—the desire to see Seth again or genuine need for work—the following morning Jet tumbled unwillingly out of bed, made several cups of very strong coffee and began to rummage doubtfully through her clothes.

If Daisy was in next door she could borrow something from her. Mentally she reviewed Daisy's wardrobe. No. She sighed. Harem trousers and caftans just wouldn't cut the mustard.

Not for the serious Mr Hagan.

Neat suits, tidy hair, and suitable business smiles he had told her. Her eyes skimmed regretfully over the red flowered skirt and came to rest on a severe little black number that her aunt had given her years ago in an effort to tame her predilection for colour. Only trouble was, Aunt Sadie's eyesight had been poor and she hadn't noticed the very long slit up the back. Jet eyed it disapprovingly, but in the end she decided it would simply have to do. She would just make sure she didn't turn her back on him—and with a clean white shirt on top she would really look quite conventional.

Promptly at nine o'clock she walked through the door of Hagan's, and the first thing she saw was the top of Seth's dark head. He was leaning over Marian's shoulder as she sat at Mary's desk, his sleeves rolled up and his fists pressed into the blotter. Both of them appeared to be studying a sheet of paper. As Jet entered, Seth raised his eyes, disturbed by the interruption. A spark flashed between them, something hot and startling.

So much for convention, thought Jet with a flutter of excitement.

And then she remembered, with a pang of dismay that hit her so hard it hurt, that Seth was already reserved, very permanently, by the hostile blonde glaring up at her from beneath the shelter of his tough and muscular arm.

CHAPTER THREE

'AH! Miss Faraway.' Marian's voice snapped out at her before Seth could—or would—say anything. 'We've just had a report from Mr Mellor.'

'Kellaway,' said Jet. 'Yes, I thought you might have.'

'Is that all you can say?' Marian's blue eyes were flat, as if they were glazed with plastic, but behind the protective shield Jet detected something smouldering and vindictive.

'No. At least—I'm sorry things didn't work out—but—have *you* ever tried to work for Mr Mellor?'

Jet wasn't looking at Marian when she spoke, but at the impassive face of Seth Hagan. And for a moment the mask cracked, and she saw a glimmer of what looked like understanding.

'Miss Takeaway, that has *nothing* to do with the case. You worked for us for just three days, and already we've had to let you go.' The clipped, chilly voice was bright with triumph and, encouraged by a giggle from the back of the room, it went on smugly, 'Really, I'm not surprised, of course. I knew as soon as I saw you that——'

'Marian.' Seth's deep baritone cut through Marian's brittle tirade like a hammer shattering glass as he turned to his secretary and, with heavy eyebrows at an angle which fascinated Jet, asked sternly, 'What's the matter, Marian? This is hardly the first time we've lost an employee after only three days' work. In fact, if I remember rightly, the record

was forty seconds...' He paused, seeming to rec-
ollect that Jet and his staff were listening, and that
Mary, the receptionist, was advancing into the room
with three cups of coffee clasped precariously in
her hands. 'Never mind. I'll deal with Miss
Kellaway.' He glanced at Jet and jerked his head
peremptorily at his office.

She felt her hackles rise immediately, then noticed that Marian's face was very red as she rose
hastily from her borrowed chair to stalk rigidly into
her office.

Jet smiled to herself and her ire dissolved instantly as once again she found herself plodding
through Marian's sanctum in the wake of Seth's
very satisfactory back. As she passed Marian's desk
and saw the blonde secretary's eyes narrow, she felt
a momentary discomfort—because somewhere deep
down she could almost sympathise with Seth's indignant fiancée.

Then she forgot all about the gorgon as Seth
turned around to face her and motioned her into a
chair.

Déjà vu. I've been here before, she thought irrationally as Seth's clear brown eyes settled once
more on her anxious face. But the eyes were almost
steely now and steel wasn't meant to be brown—
and Jet remembered that he had threatened to 'deal
with' her.

She decided she would deal with him before he
got the chance.

'I really am sorry about Mr Mellor,' she told him
sincerely, smiling at him with all the charm she
could muster—and unknowingly provoking a quite
unexpected sensation in his chest.

'So you should be.'

'Yes, but...' The smile broadened and Seth found himself hard put to it not to return it. 'You see, he would keep quoting proverbs at me, and he waited outside the lift with a stopwatch. It wasn't as though I wasn't doing the job. He didn't tell you I was a poor worker, did he?'

'No. He said you were cheeky and disrespectful—which I don't find hard to believe.'

'Oh.' Jet looked crestfallen, and again Seth felt that melting sensation in his chest. 'I suppose I was cheeky. But honestly, it's not possible to be respectful about that man. Don't you see...?' She hesitated and her voice trailed off. What was the use? Mr. Hagan was much too complacent to understand.

But she was wrong. To his own exasperation, Seth did see. All too clearly. Several perfectly competent employees had recently refused to work with Joe, and it was hardly surprising that this lovely breath of spring—even in businesslike black and white—should find it hard to put up with his pettiness. Seth sighed inwardly. Joe would probably have to go. This business with Jet was really the last straw. But meanwhile he must settle the matter at hand. And there was certainly no point in letting this beautiful butterfly think he approved of her volatile reaction to Joe. Because he didn't. He preferred women who thought things out sensibly and logically before they acted. As Marian always had— at least, she had until Jet had appeared on the scene, he qualified with a vague bewilderment.

He opened his mouth to tell Jet that, although he appreciated that Joe could be a difficult man to please, it was really no excuse for disrespect—and instead found himself smiling resignedly as he suggested that she might be interested in a job with Leighton Boatworks.

He was rewarded with the most dazzling smile he had ever seen as Jet rose unconsciously to her feet and leaned across his desk with her small palms pressed flat against the smoothly polished wood.

'Oh, thank you.' She beamed at him, completely forgetting her earlier resentment. 'Whatever it is, I'd love it.'

Seth stared up at her, noting that her perfectly shaped nose was very close to his own. He cleared his throat and leaned as far back as he could.

'Miss Kellaway,' he said drily, 'your enthusiasm does you credit. But before accepting *any* job, it's advisable to find out what's involved. A little sober reflection...'

'I never reflect soberly,' Jet grinned at him. 'If I did, I might not take it.'

He could see that she was half laughing at him, but behind the sparkling dark eyes he thought he saw a shadow—a shadow which only partly hid past hurts and disappointments. Jet might be a butterfly, he decided, but at some time in her life those bright wings had been badly singed. He was almost certain of it.

Then she leaned even further towards him, and he said quickly, 'All right. If you're sure. The job with Leighton Boatworks begins tomorrow morning. They need someone to fibreglass boats. It's a fairly routine job, I understand, but the pay's not all that bad.'

'That's all I need to hear. Thank you again, Mr Hagan.'

Seth nodded and passed her a slip of paper bearing the address of her new job. A moment later she straightened her shoulders and swung jauntily towards the door. Behind her Seth's eyes widened in unwilling appreciation as his gaze fell on the revealing slit of her very well-fitting black skirt.

The door closed behind her and he expelled his breath slowly, reaching automatically for a cigarette. Then he shook his head irritably and slammed the flat of his hand sharply on top of his desk. Damn that extraordinarily disturbing young woman. What *was* it with her—quite apart from that outrageous vision of her legs—that kept interfering with his normally ordered thoughts? He muttered under his breath, stabbed out his cigarette and immediately lit another.

The following Monday Seth found himself going through the same performance. For the *third* time in a week, he reflected grimly.

Once again Jet had just swung out of his office— and once again he had provided her with the address of a new employer. The Bagley Paper Bag Company. And if something goes wrong with *this* one, he decided even more grimly, Miss Jet Kellaway can jet permanently in any direction she chooses, as long as it's out of my life.

The Leighton Boatworks job had proved a complete disaster, because Jet had learned too late that she was allergic to the fumes of the fibreglassing process—and had had to be carried almost senseless from the plant. As there had been no way Seth could hold that against her, he had sent her along to a local rope manufacturer. That had been a disaster, too, because Jet had walked out indignantly after her first lunch-break when she discovered that the lunch-room was festooned with pin-ups of nude or near-nude men in improbably acrobatic poses.

'And what's wrong with that?' Seth had asked before he could stop himself—and before common sense returned and it occurred to him that he didn't like the idea of Jet munching fishpaste sandwiches surrounded by lewd posters any more than she did.

'Nothing,' Jet had responded provocatively as he started to retract his words. 'I just don't find muscle-bound wrestlers in the raw particularly appealing. Puts me off my lunch.'

With an effort Seth refrained from asking her what she did find appealing. Instead he stared at her repressively, the cleft in his chin more apparent than ever. Then he saw her wide mouth curl up enchantingly at the corners—and he found himself smiling back.

'All right.' He gave in resignedly. 'I'll give you just one more chance. And if you make a mess of this one, butterfly, I promise you I shall personally pick you up and throw you out of my office—permanently.' He grinned and added thoughtfully, 'An action which I think my fiancée would heartily approve.'

'I don't doubt it,' said Jet, grinning too. 'All the same...' She put her head on one side and pursed her lips reflectively. 'No, I don't really think I see you in the caveman role—although the idea's not without its possibilities.'

'You bet your life it's not. Don't try me too far, Miss Kellaway.'

Jet glanced quickly at Seth's mouth, which was no longer smiling, and assured him that she wouldn't.

The following morning she reported smartly at eight o'clock to the Bagley Paper Bag Company and was set to work stacking and packing bags.

Four days later, after a telephone call from Jet's new boss, Seth decided to pay a visit to Bagley Bags to see what was going on for himself. When Marian asked him why he was leaving early—she had been tiresomely interested in his every movement lately— he told her he was going to the moon and slammed the door loudly behind him.

But when he arrived at his destination, for a moment he thought he really must be in outer space—except space was supposed to be quiet, and until he was issued with earplugs the noise of the bag machines was enough to deafen him for life.

Mr Bagley, the owner, stood beside Seth on the factory floor and gestured at a dark-haired figure in a blue overall who was gyrating madly in front of a machine which disgorged rapid-fire paper bags.

As the bags shot out on her right side, Jet gathered them into stacks. Then she piled them on a steel shelf in front of her and, when the pile reached sufficient height, released a press which came down and squashed the whole collection into a bundle which she taped together and slid on to a moving belt to her left. At least, that was what was supposed to happen, Seth gathered.

In fact, as Jet struggled gamely to keep up, and the machine continued to spew a never-ending stream of brown rectangles, it was obvious that the bags had won the day. To top off the confusion, Jet's rather ungainly bundles invariably burst open as she slid them on to the belt.

Seth stood quietly for about two minutes, watching her, and by that time the floor was covered in paper, and Jet, as she jumped wildly from one foot to the other like a genetically deranged grasshopper, was rapidly disappearing beneath a sea of victorious bags.

'See what I mean?' groaned Mr Bagley despairingly. 'I'm afraid she just won't do, Hagan.'

Seth sighed and shook his head. 'No,' he replied loudly, his mouth quirking suspiciously. 'I'm afraid she won't, will she?'

'I'll get them to turn off the machine before it eats her,' yelled back Mr Bagley, scurrying away.

'Might not be a bad thing if it did,' muttered Seth, who was beginning to see the implications of a once-again-jobless Jet, whom he had promised to hurl bodily from his office if she asked him for yet another job. And if I give in again, he thought ruefully, Marian will have me barbecued for breakfast.

Then he caught sight of Jet standing forlornly in front of the now silent machine, surrounded by bags, and pushing a lock of dark hair wearily away from her eyes.

To hell with Marian, he decided. This pathetic child needs cheering up.

Not stopping to reflect that there was nothing remotely paternal about his reaction to the tall, slim figure drooping among the bags, and that Jet was certainly no child, pathetic or otherwise, he strode across the floor and caught her by the arm.

Jet looked up slowly, and her eyes when they encountered his were tired and desperately bewildered.

'Don't say it,' she said dully, tugging her earplugs awkwardly off her head. 'I've made a mess of things with a vengeance this time, haven't I?'

'You have,' agreed Seth, his brown eyes giving nothing away, but appearing to Jet to be fixed on her with contempt.

And suddenly her despair and weariness lifted as a wave of dizzying resentment washed over her. Who did this man think he was, anyway? Judge, jury and—executioner, all rolled into one? What did *he* know about being out of work and living on bread and peanut butter for weeks? What did he know about being young and vulnerable and falling in love with the wrong man and somehow being unable to get your life back on track? But of course he wouldn't know, would he? Or care. She had thought once before that he reminded her of Gino. Now she was sure he was almost a carbon copy. Only this time she wasn't going to be the dumb ingenue who fell for the handsome bastard.

'Let me go,' she spat, wrenching her arm furiously away. 'I'm not some piece of baggage you can manhandle—and I'm not your frozen cold fiancée either, so please keep your hands to yourself.'

As Seth uttered a word which Jet had not expected to hear from his carefully controlled lips, she added sharply, 'I suppose you came over here for an afternoon's entertainment. Well, I hope you've had a good laugh.'

But, as she turned on her heel and sped away from him towards the exit, it occurred to her briefly that she had been wrong about his eyes being contemptuous. Whatever they had reflected earlier, at the moment they were blazingly, almost frighteningly angry. Funny, that. She had thought he was too calculating for so much emotion. Not that it mattered now, because she wouldn't be seeing him again anyway. She supposed she ought to say goodbye to Mr Bagley, but what was the point when he obviously intended to sack her?

She was marching so fast along the pavement, with her eyes fixed scowlingly on the ground, that she didn't see the dark green Volvo pull up to the kerb beside her, and by the time she became aware of it a large hand had reached out and clamped around her wrist.

'Get in,' Seth ordered peremptorily.

'No, I...'

'I said get in.'

Afterwards, she never knew what prompted her to obey him—embarrassment at the interested stares they were attracting probably, along with just plain weariness—but somehow she found herself sinking on to the the passenger seat as the door of the Volvo was slammed decisively closed behind her.

'All right, *baggage*,' Seth's voice bit out at her. 'I've had all I'm going to take from you. For a start, you can leave Marian out of it. She's got more cool common sense in her little finger than you have in your entire delightful body—which I am not even remotely interested in manhandling. And for your information I can find better ways to pass an afternoon than watching you make an idiot of yourself—and my agency.'

'Oh,' began Jet, 'you utterly unspeakable...' Then she stopped as she saw that the face which she had always thought of as reserved and passionless was suffused with angry colour—and those wonderful brown eyes were still blazing with fury—at her.

'Oh,' she said again, much more quietly.

After that, she didn't say anything for a while, because as she looked away from him through the window, unwilling to meet his hot, accusing stare, it came to her that of course he was quite right. He had found her job after job, which through no fault of his had gone wrong, and he had received precious little thanks from her—and probably a great deal of trouble from his clients. And to suggest that he would be juvenile enough to be entertained by her ineptitude was indeed the crowning insult. As for her reference to Marian—that had been inexcusable.

Jet gulped and turned back towards him.

His face had returned to its normal attractive complexion now, and the eyes which had blazed with anger were distant and withdrawn.

'I'm sorry,' she said very softly, her voice shaking with remorse. 'You've been very kind, and I shouldn't have said those things, of course. I know they're not true.' She shook her head. 'I don't know why I did.'

'The battle of the bags got you down, I expect,' suggested Seth with surprising sympathy. Jet started to smile her gratitude—and then he spoiled it by adding in a maddeningly patronising tone, 'You must learn to control your temper when things don't go your way.'

Jet opened her mouth to tell him that things rarely went her way, and who was he to talk about temper after the demonstration he had just given? Then she decided it wasn't worth it. He was not going to change his attitude because of anything *she* said—and, anyway, she didn't want to fight with him any more. Especially as now, incredibly, his hand was resting on her shoulder and his thumb was very gently moving across her neck.

Jet drew in her breath, astounded at the swirl of delicious sensations cascading through her body. Patronising Seth Hagan might be, but had he any idea what he could do to a woman's libido?

She stared at him, speechless, her eyes straying to the muscle which moved involuntarily in his powerful neck—and she decided that he knew very well exactly what he was doing.

She pulled away from him and leaned against the door.

'What's the matter, butterfly?' His voice was a low, hypnotic stroking. 'I'm not going to pin you to a board.'

'To add me to your collection? No, I suppose you're not.' Jet struggled to keep her own voice steady as she added, 'Anyway, I'm not a butterfly.'

'Aren't you? And I don't have a collection.'

'Don't you? And no, I'm not.'

'No?' he mused thoughtfully, his thumb continuing to do strange things to her psyche. 'No, perhaps you're not.'

'Well—only an unintentional one,' admitted Jet with a rueful smile.

Seth laughed, his anger apparently forgotten. 'Right,' he agreed softly. 'My unintentional butterfly, that's you.'

'But I'm *not* yours,' Jet contradicted automatically.

Seth's thumb stopped stroking.

'No,' he responded gruffly, both hands now tightly gripped on the wheel. 'No. Of course you're not.'

Jet stared at him, noting the way his shoulder muscles bunched against the stark white of his shirt. And she wondered why he suddenly seemed vulnerable—and why, for one wild, ridiculous moment, she wished she had not denied that she was his.

Then sanity returned and she said quickly, 'I have to go now, Mr Hagan. Thank you for all you've tried to do for me.' She smiled wryly. 'You might not believe it, but I really am very grateful.'

She reached for the door—and found her exit blocked solidly by his arm as he stretched across her and caught the handle firmly in his hand.

Brown eyes changed to gold and locked with deeper brown. His face was very close to hers and she could feel his warm breath on her cheek. For the first time she was aware of the smell of him— spicy, male, and very seductive. And then, unbelievably, she felt the feather-light touch of his incredible lips on her mouth—before he pulled back from her and said, so matter-of-factly that she thought she must be dreaming, 'You're not going anywhere, Miss Kellaway. Except out to dinner with me.'

'What?' Jet gaped at him. 'What are you talking about, Mr Hagan?'

'Food. You know, that delicious stuff that keeps body and soul together—and which you've had far too little of lately, judging from the flesh—or lack of it—on your bones.'

'Thanks,' said Jet sourly. 'You're a great ego booster, Mr Hagan. And for the last time, I *don't* need your precious charity.'

'*Don't* you?' replied Seth equably. 'You know, for once I'm beginning to agree with you. Just at the moment I think there's something that might do you a lot more good than food.'

Jet decided she didn't at all care for the way his hand slapped at his thigh as his eyes fastened speculatively on that part of her anatomy which Uncle Joe had found so useful when she misbehaved. She edged away from him and reached again for the door.

'Mr Hagan...' she began warily.

'Oh, for pete's sake, stop Mr Haganing me.' Seth's eyes stopped speculating and became positively decisive. Jet edged as far away from him as she could. 'Don't you think we're past the "Mr Hagan" stage?' he snapped.

Well, they certainly would be if he did what he was obviously contemplating. She swallowed and nodded uncomfortably. 'Yes—I suppose... All right, Mr...' She stopped and smiled a little shakily. 'What did you say your name was, Mr Hagan?'

'Oh, for pete's sake,' said Seth again. But this time he started to laugh. 'It's Seth. Seth Robert Cornelius, to be distressingly accurate—but try to forget the Cornelius.'

'I should think so,' agreed Jet feelingly, as she began to relax again.

'Mm. Now tell me why you're called Jet.'

'Well, it's Jetta, really. My mother was Danish.'

Seth shook his head. 'Danish? I'd never have believed it.'

'Because of my colouring, you mean? I know. I used to dream I was a changeling princess from a South Sea Island and that my parents had kidnapped me at birth—until Aunt Sadie told me no one in their right mind would kidnap *me*, and that in my case I got my hair from my father.'

'And was he from a South Sea Island?' Seth mocked her gently.

'No. Cardiff.'

Seth laughed. 'Is Wales not exotic enough for you, then?'

'Well, I suppose it can be,' said Jet doubtfully. 'Caernarvon has a nice romantic ring to it.'

Seth didn't answer, but for a moment there was a slightly confused look in his eyes. 'Romantic...' he began. Then he stopped. 'All right, princess. Let's cut the conversation and go and get some food.'

'I told you. I don't want food.'

'Well, I do. And I don't care what you want, you're getting it.'

Jet felt her temper flare again, and then die down as quickly. She was really too tired to quarrel.

'Trying the caveman stuff again?' she asked drily. 'It doesn't go over big with me, you know.'

'Oh, *doesn't* it?' he taunted. 'Well, it doesn't go over big with me either as a matter of fact, but if it's the only way I can shut you up and take you for a decent meal...'

'I'm not the Christmas turkey, and I *don't* need fattening up, if that's what you're trying to imply.'

'It's not. And you need no encouragement whatever to be a turkey. I'm trying to ask you out, if you'd just stop fighting me long enough to listen.'

'Oh.' Jet felt as if the air had suddenly been sucked from her lungs. 'Why *don't* you ask me, then?'

Seth turned his body towards her, and for a moment he looked so explosive that she thought he wanted to hit her. Then he expelled a long, controlled breath, placed a large hand tightly over her left shoulder and said through nearly clenched teeth, 'Will you have dinner with me tonight, Jet Kellaway? If it isn't too much to ask.'

'It isn't. Thank you. Yes, I will.' Jet's voice came out almost in a squeak, and she couldn't understand why she felt a sudden ridiculous urge to sing.

Seth's mouth relaxed slowly and he nodded, his face now disconcertingly blank.

'Right. Let's go.' He released her shoulder abruptly and started up the car.

'I have to change first,' said Jet faintly. 'I can't go out like this.'

He glanced quickly at her blue overall. 'No. I suppose you can't. I'll drive you home, then, and wait for you while you change.'

'All right.' Jet was long past any inclination to argue.

But it wasn't until the Volvo pulled up outside her basement that she remembered she couldn't have dinner with Seth, after all. Because he had no right to ask her.

'Miss Sinclair,' she murmured, jumping from the car before he could stop her. 'I can't have dinner with you, Seth. Your fiancée wouldn't like it a bit.'

CHAPTER FOUR

'MARIAN?' For a moment Seth's face registered only disbelief. Then that gave way to half-amused consternation. 'Do you know, for a moment I'd almost forgotten her?'

'So it seems,' replied Jet severely, ignoring the fact that she too had forgotten Seth's efficient and organising fiancée. But then, she had a right to forget. Seth hadn't.

She took a deep breath and pulled the blue overall more closely around her body, feeling suddenly chilly in the cool spring air. 'Anyway, now that you've remembered, Mr...Seth, I'd better say thank you, again—and goodbye.'

'Don't talk nonsense.' Now he too was levering himself out of the car. As he straightened and slammed the door behind him, Jet sighed and thought once more what an excitingly lean and attractive man he was. Tempting, really. Yes . . . But, of course, she mustn't be tempted, must she?

He was walking towards her now with an odd little smile on his lips. 'Come on, butterfly. Change your clothes and then we can be on our way.'

'But . . . Seth, we can't. Your Marian . . .'

'Never mind Marian. She's my problem, not yours. I promised you a meal, and you're damn well going to get one. Besides—this dinner is strictly business.'

'Business?' Jet eyed him doubtfully. 'What sort of business?'

'You'll find out over dinner.'

'Oh.' Jet hesitated. She was curious now. And in spite of herself—and in spite of Marian—she knew she wanted to spend the evening with Seth. He might be patronising, and much too sure of himself, but today he had actually shown signs of being quite promisingly human.

She made up her mind. He had said strictly business. Marian couldn't object to that. Besides, Marian was a snooty, self-satisfied gorgon, and it would do her good to object.

As she preceded Seth into her living-room, feeling more conscious than ever of its shabbiness, she reminded herself that Marian's personality had nothing to do with the issue. No, of course it hadn't. Still . . . he really *had* said business . . .

Seth lowered himself easily into the brown tweed chair, stretched his legs in front of him and told her to hurry up and change.

'I wish you'd stop telling me what to do,' Jet grumbled, pulling her overall off and tossing it carelessly over the divan.

Seth grinned. 'Do it then, and I won't have to.'

'Do what?'

'Take off those faded jeans and put on something respectable.'

'And where am I supposed to do that?' asked Jet tartly, irritated by his disparaging reference to her clothes.

'What do you mean?'

'In case you haven't noticed, apart from a minuscule bathroom, I live and sleep and cook in this apology for a room, which was advertised as compact and easy to clean. And I'm really not interested in doing a striptease for you, Seth Hagan.'

His grin broadened and a provocative gleam lit his eye. 'Aren't you, now? That's too bad. Perhaps some other time...'

'And perhaps not,' said Jet firmly. 'Now, would you kindly turn your back?'

Seth stared at her and the gleam turned suddenly opaque. He shook his head as if trying to clear his field of vision. 'Right,' he said, standing up quickly. 'Don't be long, though, or I won't guarantee not to look.'

Jet glanced at him suspiciously. That didn't sound much like the severe and collected man she thought she knew.

As he turned to face the damp and peeling wall, Seth was having similar thoughts himself. What was the matter with him? Forgetting about Marian— who most certainly *would* be a problem when she heard about tonight—telling Jet he wanted to discuss business, when the only possible business he could have with her must be highly suspect. Unless... Oh, lord. Unless, of course, he offered her another job. And now he had no choice, had he? He closed his eyes, shutting out a pattern of ugly brown stains, and when he opened them again Jet was standing in front of him, looking warm and bright and alive in a dress of worn but cheerful canary-coloured wool. He blinked and returned her smile cautiously. Then, taking a very long breath, he seized her arm and marched her briskly out into the cooling April dusk.

'You forgot to bring a coat,' he remarked half an hour later, as the car came to a halt outside a small Ukrainian restaurant in North Vancouver.

'I didn't. You hustled me out so quickly, I didn't have time to grab one. Anyway, I thought I wouldn't need it in the car.'

Seth shook his head. 'Don't you ever think ahead?' he asked resignedly, as he opened the door and pulled her up beside him. 'You might have known it would get cold later on.'

Jet felt a familiar twinge of annoyance. Mr Know-it-all was doing it to her again. 'I told you,' she snapped. 'You didn't give me time.'

'Of course I did——' he started to contradict her. And then she shivered, and he stopped abruptly. Here was this too thin, hungry-looking girl shivering in the dusk without a coat—and he was lecturing her on the virtues of forethought and common sense. Quickly he leaned inside the car, pulled his dark grey jacket from the back seat and swung it around her shoulders.

'There,' he said, one arm holding her against him as they walked towards the open restaurant door. 'That should solve the problem.'

Yes, thought Jet, leaning comfortably against him and amazed at how much she liked the feel of him at her side. It'll solve one problem all right. But, as his arm tightened almost imperceptibly and a jolt of something sensual and unexpected lurched much too pleasantly inside her stomach, she was not at all sure that his solution hadn't given rise to a different set of difficulties altogether. She glanced at his profile, but as usual he looked calm and self-contained, and the slight rigidity of his jaw she put down to his normal reserve. Inexplicably, she felt an almost overpowering urge to lift her hand to disturb that neatly combed hair. In fact, to do anything which would ruffle his smooth, smug complacency.

But they were inside the restaurant now, and as the hostess came towards them, smiling her best public smile, Seth deftly removed the jacket, shrugged it quickly over his own shoulders and smoothed her long hair carefully down her back. His fingers just brushed against her neck again, and Jet felt suddenly warm.

She felt even warmer twenty minutes later as they sat at a table by the window. She sipped gratefully at a bowl of deep red *borscht* and watched the lights of cars flash across the Lions Gate Bridge.

'Better?' asked Seth, smiling at her. There was a fire in the corner of the dimly lit room, and the reflection of the flames moved softly over his face, making it warmer, gentler—and more hypnotically sensuous than before.

'Yes,' murmured Jet. 'Much better.' She couldn't take her eyes off his lips.

'Good.' He nodded at a tall blond waiter by the door and a moment later crimson liquid was gleaming seductively in her glass. 'To the success of your next assignment from Hagan's.' Seth's voice was as seductive as the wine as he raised his glass and smiled at her over the rim.

'What?' said Jet, her own glass half-way to her lips. 'What did you say?'

'I said to your next assignment with Hagan's.' Now there was a note of resignation in his voice. A quiet note, but evident, none the less.

Jet shook her head and moved the salt-cellar mechanically across the checked cloth. 'Oh, no,' she said. 'You've done too much for me already. I don't want to ruin your company's reputation altogether. Besides...' she grinned ruefully, 'you said you'd throw me out of your office if I asked you for yet another job.'

'Yes, but you're not asking. And I suppose there's no reason why you should mess up *every* job you get—is there? Or were you hired by the competition to put me out of business?'

He saw a look of hurt flare momentarily in Jet's eyes, and was immediately, and startlingly, contrite. But before he could say anything she was replying quietly, 'No, there's no reason for my failures. They just seem to happen. At least—I suppose I'm not very good at keeping up with machinery. It always seems to end up outmanoeuvring me—like the paper bags did today. But it's not usually anything like that which goes wrong. Sometimes I think I've found a great job at last, and then the company goes bankrupt. A lot of my jobs were temporary in the first place, like looking after children, or the fish cannery. And other times, I honestly don't know what happens.' She slid the pepper-pot over beside the salt. 'People like Joe Mellor, cutbacks in staff...I don't know. I really *do* want something permanent, Seth. I used to want desperately to teach. The younger ones, you know, when they're still all bright and eager to learn...' For a moment Seth saw her eyes light up in the firelight, and then her voice trailed off and her head fell forward so that her long hair drifted across the empty soup bowl.

He reached across and pushed the stray wisp behind her ear. And when Jet looked up he thought he saw moisture in her eyes.

'Look,' he said quietly, 'you know what I think? You're a maddening, frustrating, irresponsible—

and very beautiful young woman. But I don't think there's anything congenitally wrong with your brain. Maybe you've just had bad luck, but it seems to me—and I don't understand *why*—that underneath that bright and breezy exterior of yours lurks a woman with a complete lack of faith in herself. It's probably been obvious in every job you've ever held. You've expected to fail, and so of course you have. Now, why don't you get a grip on yourself, stop all the nonsense and learn to put up with the Joe Mellors of this world? Take this job I'm offering you, and begin some education courses at night. When you've saved enough money, you can start at university full-time.'

Two steaming plates of *perogies* and *holopchi* appeared on the table at that moment, along with rich mushroom sauce and sour cream, so it was a few minutes before Jet was able to reply. When she did, Seth saw that her eyes were almost bemused, and she was staring at him as if he had told her to climb a rainbow—though all he had actually done was point out that her ambitions were not wholly unrealistic.

Then the bemused look faded and she closed her eyes briefly. When she opened them again she said irritably, 'And you know what I think, Mr Freud? That underneath that high and mighty exterior of yours lurks an amateur psychiatrist just waiting to break out. In fact, I think he *has* broken out—and you would be doing all us psychos and weirdos a favour if you'd put him back in the closet where he belongs.'

'Ouch.' Seth winced, and his fingers tapped ominously on the edge of the table.

Jet pulled herself together and added hastily, 'But thank you very much, anyway. Of course I'll take the job. I can't afford not to, can I?'

'Charmingly put. Your graciousness overwhelms me,' he drawled.

'Oh, dear.' Unconsciously Jet raised her hand and put it to her mouth. 'That *was* awful of me, wasn't it? I know you meant to be helpful.

'But you don't like people analysing your motives. Especially not amateur psychiatrists like me.'

'I suppose I don't. And anyway I *do* have faith in myself—and I'm not irresponsible.' She smiled tentatively. 'That's why I'm going to make a fantastic success of this job—if you'll still let me have it.'

He gave her a long, searching look, and for a moment she had the feeling he could see right through her. Then he smiled without much amusement, and said that she'd better be fantastic because if she let him down again he'd be sorely tempted to run her through a Bagley Bag machine.

'But you won't let me down,' he said firmly, when she showed signs of wanting to giggle. 'I don't know why it is, butterfly, but *I* have faith in you.'

She put down her fork, and he placed his hand briefly over hers. His touch was an aphrodisiac, dizzying and disorientating, so that for a moment she no longer knew where she was. Then he was picking up his knife and fork to continue his meal, as though nothing had changed between them.

Swallowing hard, and with bright colour still lingering on her cheeks, Jet followed his example.

'You must like Ukrainian food,' she said after a while, because the silence between them was making her uncomfortable and she needed something to say.

'Yes, I do. We had a Ukrainian housekeeper when I was growing up. I used to help her cut the dough for the *perogies*.' He grinned. 'But that's not why I brought you here. I thought you needed something hot and filling.'

'Whether I liked it or not?'

'More or less.' He gestured at her almost empty plate and added teasingly, 'But I think you'd have tucked away buttered hiking boots if they had happened to be on the menu.'

Jet laughed. 'I wouldn't. I'm allergic to butter.'

'Liar.' He pointed a finger at the thick pat of butter on her side-plate.

Jet ignored him and polished off her last little cheese and potato-filled dumpling. Then she took a satisfying bite of *holopchi*. 'Did you help your housekeeper with the cabbage rolls, too?' she asked. 'Aunt Sadie wouldn't let *me* in the kitchen. She said I was a menace.'

'Mm. You probably were. Mrs Foychuk said the same about my cabbage rolls. They always came apart. Who's Aunt Sadie?'

'Aha. So you haven't *always* been perfect,' Jet taunted, unable to resist getting some of her own back. But when she saw the retaliatory glint in his eyes she added quickly, 'Aunt Sadie is my father's sister. She and Uncle Joe brought me up. My father drowned in a boating accident when I was three, and after that my mother—just gave up. She died of pneumonia six months later.'

There. Now they were over that hurdle. Seth knew as much of her history as she wanted him to know, and they could talk about something else.

But Seth thought differently. He was looking at her with an expression of growing comprehension and, when she saw the sympathy in his eyes, quite suddenly she wanted to throw a plate at him—or burst into tears on the table. But that was something she rarely did. She had cried inside about the parents she had never known, for more years than she could remember. But she had discovered early that all tears ever earned her from Uncle Joe and Aunt Sadie was a sore bottom or banishment to her room. So crying was a luxury she had learned to live without.

'Do you remember your parents?' Seth was asking her gently.

'No.' That should be brief enough to discourage him.

It wasn't.

'But your aunt and uncle were good to you, of course.'

'Of course nothing,' Jet snapped—because she didn't want to talk about her past, and she didn't know how else to stop him probing.

'They weren't good to you?' For once his face was not impassive, and his concern was harder to bear than his superiority.

He picked up her hand and held it. And suddenly, for the first time in years, she felt her defences crumble. And then, to her horror, she found herself blurting out everything—or almost everything. She told him how her aunt and uncle had resented her intrusion into their tight little family circle. There hadn't been much money, and she was just another mouth to feed. A whining, complaining mouth at first, they told her, because she had lost her parents and was too young to understand why. Oh, they had seen to her material needs, of course, and tried to do what they conceived of as their duty. But they couldn't help it that their love was all for their own two quiet blonde daughters, and that there was not much left over for the dark-haired, active, vocal little niece. Soon she had learned to hide her enthusiasms and to cover her hurts with a breezy confidence she was often far from feeling. Seth had been right about that. But she didn't tell him so. She didn't need to because he knew already.

And there was something else she wasn't going to tell him, either. Something she never talked about to anyone. Something—and someone—who for seven years she had been trying hard to forget.

'Poor little waif.' Seth broke in softly on her reverie, and the gentleness in his tone made her clench her hands beneath the table and blink her eyes quickly to stop any tears from spilling over.

'I'm not a waif,' she mumbled, staring desperately at her plate. 'And I don't need any of your phoney sympathy, either.'

Seth sighed and shook his head. 'Still a prickly waif,' he remarked somewhat less gently. 'Don't worry, you're not going to get any sympathy. How about crêpes Suzette instead?'

Jet passed a hand surreptitiously over her eyes. 'You're still determined to fatten me for Christmas, aren't you?'

'Not really. If you'd stop throwing quills at me, porcupine, you'd be quite a nice armful as you are.'

'Well, you won't be finding out, will you?' she replied crossly.

'You never know.'

'Yes, I do. You're engaged.'

'Mm, so I am.' He drawled the words out lazily, but Jet could have sworn that for a moment there was a genuinely surprised look on his face.

When the crêpes came, Jet's eyes grew big with anticipation, which made Seth start to laugh. 'If I can't win your heart any other way, I believe I might do it with food,' he said lightly.

'So now I'm greedy, as well as frustrating and irresponsible,' scoffed Jet, carefully ignoring his reference to her heart.

His features seemed to soften then, the harsh lines wiped away, as he replied in that very deep voice which did something odd to her senses, 'No, my love. Not greedy. Just very hungry, that's all.'

His love? What did he mean by that? She stared fixedly at an embroidered picture on the wall and made sure she didn't meet his eyes. Of course he meant nothing whatever by it. Some men used endearments as easily as they breathed—and Seth was undoubtedly one of those. Besides, he had probably had plenty of practice. Engaged to the gorgon he might be, but there must have been plenty of other women in his life. With a face and physique like that... Yes, well, she'd been into that already, hadn't she?

The coffee arrived. Seth lit a cigarette and asked casually, 'With all the time you must spend looking for work, do you ever manage a social life as well?' It seemed an innocuous enough question, but from the sudden tension in his shoulders Jet had a feeling it wasn't as detached as it appeared.

'Of course I do.' She laughed, a little bleakly. 'I go to the coffee bars with John and Daisy next door, and sometimes to parties. I swim down at Jericho

Beach in the summer, visit old schoolfriends—I grew up in Vancouver, you know—anything that doesn't cost much money...'

'Hmm.' His blunt fingers were tapping out a rhythm on the table as he leaned back in his chair and studied her face appraisingly, as though he didn't quite believe what he was hearing. 'No dancing, no movies, ballet or nightclubs? No romantic dinners in rooftop restaurants? You surprise me, butterfly. Don't you have a boyfriend?' The brown eyes were suddenly very bright and keen.

'It's none of your business, *Mr* Hagan, but as a matter of fact I don't. And that's just the way I like it.' Before he had a chance to ask more awkward questions, she went on quickly, 'But since we're getting personal, is that what you and Marian do? Go dancing, kick up your heels at nightclubs—and have long, lingering dinners in the moonlight? Because if it is,' she added pertly, 'I must have misjudged you entirely.'

Seth stopped looking casual, curious—and faintly patronising, and leaned forward with his fists locked together on the table.

'Oh, must you?' he responded grimly. 'So you imagined I sit up there in my ivory tower all day making executive decisions, reading the *Financial Times*, checking the stock-market—and taking Marian for the occasional sober business lunch...'

'Well, don't you?'

'You little...' He groaned, and a look of frustration crossed his face—but after a moment it was followed by a grin of what had to be pure self-mockery. 'Yes, I suppose I do—sometimes.'

'I knew it,' Jet crowed. Then, as another, somehow less pleasing idea occurred to her, 'But you can't always have been so—serious.'

'You think not?'

'Well, I . . .'

'Oh, don't worry.' He sounded exasperated now. 'I've committed my share of youthful indiscretions. Happily, all well in the past. And now I've found a sensible, clear-headed, highly efficient woman who shares my goals, and values a well-ordered home. I'm very lucky.' He spoke so emphatically that Jet wondered if he was trying to convince himself.

'Sense, clear-headedness, efficiency? Is that all you want from your marriage, Seth?' she asked.

He heard the amusement in her voice, but he knew she wasn't really teasing, and suddenly he was quite astonishingly angry. He also knew there was no reason for the anger he was having such a job to control.

'Finish your coffee. It's time I took you home,' he said curtly.

Jet saw the set look on his face and the way the sensual lips had hardened into a line—and was surprised to find she felt instantly bereft. She gulped her coffee so quickly that it almost choked her, and shortly afterwards they were speeding across the Lions Gate Bridge.

'You're going too fast,' she told him sharply, after he had totally ignored her for several minutes. 'It's a beautiful night, and I'd like to sit back and enjoy it. Besides, speeding isn't *sensible*, is it?'

When Seth's only response was a gruff order to 'shut up', Jet knew she had won a very minor victory.

He drew up at her house with a surprising squeal of brakes, leaned across her, pushed open the door and told her to get out.

'Where are your manners, *Mr* Hagan?' Jet asked sweetly. 'And you haven't yet told me about my new job.'

Seth swore under his breath, and strode quickly around to her side of the car.

'And now will you condescend to get out?' he asked silkily, bowing low over her hand as he helped her to stand up.

'Certainly, sir.' Head held high, Jet minced ahead of him, fumbled for her key and was closing the door very satisfyingly in his face when she felt his hand close ungently around her arm.

'Oh, no, you don't,' he said smoothly—too smoothly. 'There's a job to discuss. Remember? And we have some other unfinished business as well.'

'What sort of business?' asked Jet suspiciously, trying to step away from him, and finding she couldn't because he had followed her inside and was shutting the door purposefully behind him. His hand was still wrapped around her wrist and his nose was about two inches from her own.

'This sort of business.'

Suddenly both his arms were locked tightly behind her back, and when she tried to move she couldn't. And then she didn't want to because his shining dark brown head had lowered over hers and his mouth was pressing against her lips, parting them, moving in erotic exploration. Somewhere beneath the tumultuous sensations in her body she knew that she should stop him—if she could—that this was wrong and only his form of retribution.

But she didn't want to stop him because every moment since the instant she had first seen him staring out of his office window had been leading up to this. Not meaning to, but unable to prevent herself, she wound her arms around his neck—and he responded by pulling her closer so that every part of her body was moulded against his. His tongue pressed between her teeth and she curled her fingers in the hair which barely touched his neck.

And then he released her, so suddenly that she staggered back against the door. She stared at him in mindless confusion, not understanding, until she caught the slight curl of his lip and saw that his brown eyes had changed to green again and that he was regarding her with something like triumph, as if all his expectations had been most satisfactorily confirmed.

And she drew herself up to her full five foot eight and said dispassionately, 'You know, Seth Hagan, your hair is really *far* too short.'

CHAPTER FIVE

'WHAT?' Seth stared at her as if his ears had badly let him down. A series of colourfully conflicting emotions passed rapidly over his face. Disbelief, indignation, outright anger, and finally, incredibly—dared she believe it?—amusement.

Then, as Jet stared at him in utter confusion, Seth threw back the glossy head she had just censured and let out a shout of uninhibited laughter.

She watched him warily, unable to take her eyes off the tough, muscular body, now shaking with mirth as his chest strained against the whiteness of his shirt.

'And you dress much too conservatively,' she added, not knowing him well enough to quit while she was ahead.

Seth stopped laughing abruptly. 'You little witch,' he said softly, moving towards her with retribution in his eye. 'You've pushed your luck too far this time, butterfly.'

'No...don't,' Jet protested, looking furtively behind her for a bolt-hole. But there was only the door, and as she groped for the handle Seth was already upon her, towing her relentlessly towards the divan which served as a bed.

'Ouch!' she shrieked, as she was pulled across his thighs with her head pressed just below his chest.

'I haven't done anything to you yet, minx. For all you damn well deserve it.' There was laughter in his voice, and Jet stopped trying to squirm and lay still. Oh, heavens, what was this man trying to do to her?

'So my hair's too short, is it?' he whispered.

'No,' gasped Jet. 'Not really...'

'And I dress too conservatively, do I?' One finger ran lingeringly down the lower part of her spine.

'No. No, you're—you're...'

'I'm what?'

'You're much too horribly attractive,' groaned Jet distractedly.

But as soon as the words were out she remembered that this had to stop. Seth *was* horribly attractive. He could be kind too, sometimes, and in spite of his sober demeanour he often made her laugh. But he didn't really approve of her and, if this went any further, by morning he would regret it. No. Wait a minute. There was something wrong about that...

Of course. It was the woman who was supposed to regret it in the morning. Not the successfully predatory hunk.

Seth was lying very still now, his eyelids lowered and one hand softly stroking her hair. And Jet, seeing her opportunity, put both hands on his chest and pushed herself to her feet. A moment later she had sprung across the room.

Seth sat up, rested his elbows on his knees and bent his head forward over his hands.

'I *must* be out of my mind,' he murmured, his voice so low that she could barely hear him.

'It's all right,' Jet whispered, her own voice very choked and thin. She turned away and pressed her cheek against the wall.

'Yes,' agreed Seth. 'It is hell, isn't it? Goodnight, Jet. Sleep well.'

Before she realised what was happening, he had swung open the door. She caught just a glimpse of a forsythia bush waving in the darkness before he disappeared into the night, and by the time she came to her senses she could hear the Volvo purring down the street.

And that's that, thought Jet resignedly as she opened an eye the next morning and saw rain spattering at her one small window high up in the wall. I'm not at all sure how it happened, but I seem to have blown away yet another job—this time before it even started.

Surprisingly, that didn't seem to matter nearly as much as the fact that she'd also blown away all hope of seeing Seth again. Or they had blown it together.

Everything might have been leading up to what had happened last night. She had no doubt of that. But it had been a culmination, not a beginning. The culmination of what had been no more than a powerful physical attraction.

She shifted restlessly in the bed. Anyway, it was probably just as well things had turned out as they had. Even without the ever-present spectre of Marian, there wasn't a hope that she and Seth could ever be more than friends—and wary friends at that. They were just too different. He wanted order and efficiency and everything in its place. She wanted—what did she want? Love, she supposed, and permanence and commitment—but with a healthy dose of chaos to keep things from getting too stale. Perhaps Seth had been right to call her a butterfly.

She stared gloomily at the bare lightbulb and thought about getting out of bed. She had just decided there wasn't much point in it, and that she might as well go back to sleep, when the telephone rang.

As she reached for it, her heart gave a sudden wild flutter.

But it wasn't Seth's voice that came cracking at her over the wires, but that of his secretary, the gorgon—and from the sound of it Marian was no happier about calling Jet than Jet was about taking the call—until she realised that Marian was phoning on Seth's instructions and that the new job was still hers, after all.

'Mr Hagan says he keeps his promises,' said Marian acidly, when Jet expressed her surprise.

'Yes,' she murmured. 'Yes, I suppose he would.'

'Naturally.'

Marian went on to explain to Jet in clipped, precise phrases just exactly what her new job would involve.

Gourmet Distributors was a large wholesale food supplier which dealt with most of the better restaurants in Vancouver—and some of the more dubious ones, too, Jet decided after she had worked in the flat concrete box near the waterfront for a week. She liked the job, and was ecstatic that for the first time in her life she could see the mountains from her window all day—when it wasn't raining.

Mr Allison, the fatherly office manager of Gourmet, appeared to approve of her, too. Her initial interview had been a mere formality, as he told her Seth's recommendation was good enough for him. That made Jet even more determined not to let him down, even though she was sure Seth would take care not to see her again.

Jet's job was to answer the telephone and connect the callers, usually distraught chefs who had just run out of caviare or Chinese chestnuts, to a salesperson who could take their order. It was also her job to operate the photocopier, the coffee machine and a particularly lethal weapon which opened letters. Jet found it frequently opened her as well. When people started to complain that their correspondence was delivered looking as though it had just come down with chicken pox, she began to take special care to slow down, and for a while she thought she had everything under control. Then the malevolent letter opener broke down altogether.

Over the next couple of days the photocopier and the coffee machine also gave up the ghost ungracefully, and Mr Allison remarked, rather testily and with much less approval than he had shown her when she started, that for insurance purposes from now on perhaps office equipment ought to be filed under 'Jetta'.

'But I'm really not in the same class as fire, flood or earthquake,' she protested.

Mr Allison, who was in no mood for flippancy, only glared at her and said he wasn't so sure.

Jet sighed. It was usually at about this point in her employment that she found herself looking for other work.

But the recalcitrant machines were repaired, and for the next week or so everything seemed to go well—or as well as was possible while she was unable to shake a vague, unhappy feeling that somehow she had lost something precious that she very much wanted to keep.

Seth had not phoned her or been near her since their last memorable evening, and as far as she knew his marriage plans must be forging ahead. It was early June now, and she had an idea he had mentioned a July wedding date. And that's just as it should be, Jet Kellaway, she told herself on more than one occasion, frustrated that she couldn't keep Seth completely out of her mind. But she was putting money in the bank these days and hoping to start a night school course in September, so there was no reason whatever to feel sorry for herself. At least, that was what she tried to believe as she worked doggedly through the long hours of each day.

It was only a few weeks later that another problem started to surface. She noticed that every time she moved, or went to the water fountain, a trio of young men from the sales department seemed to emerge out of nowhere and keep her chatting pointlessly while she tried to get back to the phones. Each time she started towards her desk, one of them would grab her arm, say 'hold on a minute' and bring up another topic of conversation—invariably not even remotely connected with the job. She knew that Midge, the relief receptionist, was getting irritated, and in the end she had to give up leaving her post at all until her lunch-break.

This worked for about two days, and then the trio moved their centre of activities to her desk. Whenever she looked up she seemed to find a young male face leering over the top of her head. It was distracting and annoying, but there wasn't much she could do about it. And then one day Mr Allison called her into his office.

'Miss Kellaway,' he began without preamble, 'this nonsense has got to stop.'

Jet gaped at him. 'Wh-what?' she stuttered.

'It has been brought to my attention,' he boomed ominously, 'that there's a disgraceful wager going the rounds in Sales.'

'Wager?' repeated Jet blankly.

'That's what I said. Are you telling me you know nothing about it?'

'Of course I don't.' Jet was beginning to get her wits back. 'Do you think you could please explain what you mean?'

'I mean,' said Mr Allison slowly and judge-mentally, 'that they're laying bets as to which one of them will...' He cleared his throat. 'Will—er— be the one to—hm——' He cleared it again. 'Get you into—er...'

'Bed?' suggested Jet coldly, her face going very pale.

Mr Allison stopped looking judgemental, and began to look almost grateful. 'Precisely.'

Jet's skin turned immediately from white to furious red, as she said in a tight voice in which the anger was barely controlled, 'You're not trying to suggest that that's *my* fault, are you, Mr Allison?'

He shook his head hastily. 'No, no, Miss Kellaway. I can hardly say that, can I? But it was suggested to me that you might have been—well— encouraging them.'

'I've been trying to *dis*courage them. Without much success,' snapped Jet indignantly.

'Yes, of course. I see. My mistake. I was told— well, never mind, I think the problem should be under control, then. I'll speak to the people involved.'

'I'd be glad if you would,' said Jet tonelessly. Why, oh, why did this always happen to her? Or if it didn't, then why did something else go wrong?

But Mr Allison was clearing his throat again. 'Miss Kellaway?'

'Yes?' What on earth could be coming now?

'Miss Kellaway—are you busy this evening?'

'No, not really. Do you have some work you want me to finish up?'

'No, no. Nothing like that. Misjudged you, I'm afraid. Like to—ah—make amends. Take you out to dinner. Hmm?'

Oh, no, surely *he* wasn't going to start too. Jet stared at him, speechless.

'Just a small token of my—appreciation,' he persisted.

Jet shook her head violently. 'No, no, I couldn't. I—I have to go now, Mr Allison. Th—thank you.'

She turned from him and fled blindly out of his office. And as she stumbled away she saw his mouth fall open and his face turn an ugly brick red.

Oh, damn, she groaned to herself as she collapsed in front of her desk. I bet that's torn it. If he meant what I thought he meant, he'll be angry— and if it was just a kindly impulse, which I'm now horribly afraid it was, he'll be embarrassed. Either way, he won't want to keep me around.

But he did keep her around, although she saw very little of him. The trio from Sales vanished abruptly from her orbit, and it was several weeks later before the axe finally fell.

Jet had stayed late to catch up on some copying, and it was growing dark when she passed the security guard at the door. She flashed her card at him without looking up, and would have passed by without even seeing who he was if a voice behind her had not called bossily, 'Hold it there, miss. I want to see your face.'

Sighing, Jet turned around—and found herself looking straight up into the mean little eyes of Joe Mellor.

'You!' he spat, taking a step towards her. 'Well, well, well, if it isn't Miss High and Flighty herself. The neat little number who managed to lose me my job.'

'What?' frowned Jet. 'I didn't ... What are you talking about, Mr Mellor?'

'Seth Hagan sacked me right after I sacked you,' he replied bitterly, 'and this security job is all I've been able to find since. You owe me something for that one, little madam—and now's as good a time as any to pay your debts.'

'I don't owe you anything,' flashed Jet angrily, stepping backwards and almost tripping over the step.

'Oh, yes, you do.' Joe caught her as she fell, and when she stumbled to her feet again she found his arm was still tightly around her waist, his fingers digging into her side until it hurt.

'Let me go,' she hissed furiously.

'Why should I?' His mouth was very close to hers now, and she could smell the sour beer odour on his breath.

'Because if you don't ...'

But the sentence was never completed because suddenly Joe's flabby lips were against hers, and his callused hand was knotted in her hair.

'Oh!' Jet tore her mouth away, shoved his chest hard with both hands and managed to pull herself away—although the stinging pain at the back of her head made her think she must have left half her scalp behind.

'You're not getting away with that, Joe Mellor,' she shouted at him, and she sprinted towards Pender Street and the bus. 'I'll report it to Mr Allison in the morning, and you'll find yourself out of work again.'

He made no attempt to follow her and, still shaking with anger, a few minutes later she was safely on her way home.

By the time she got there she was feeling a lot more subdued. It was all very well to say she would report him, but the whole thing was horribly embarrassing and she didn't relish the thought of Mr Allison's reaction when he learned that, because she had been late leaving, he would have to get a new man for the door. Especially as he had been studiously avoiding her of late and obviously would not be pleased to find her in his office—complaining.

'But it wasn't my fault,' she wailed to Daisy, when her chubby and cheerful friend came over in answer to Jet's urgent plea. 'What do you think I should *do*?'

'Do? That's easy. Report the bastard.' Daisy's plump face registered amazement that Jet could even consider anything else.

'Yes, I suppose you're right,' Jet said glumly, wilting tiredly over the kitchen sink as she filled the kettle with water.

'Of course I'm right. If he'll try it on you, he'll try it on someone else.'

'I suppose so,' agreed Jet again. 'But you see, he wanted to get even with me. He might not behave that way with someone else.'

'Don't you believe it,' said Daisy forcefully. 'Come on, Jetta. What's happened to all that Kellaway gumption and guts?'

'I don't know,' sighed Jet. 'I think I must have washed them down the drain.'

But she knew Daisy was right. She spent a restless night, and in the morning went straight to see Mr Allison.

He was frowning down at his desk, but when she walked through the door he looked up quickly.

'Ah, Miss Kellaway.' His voice was non-committal and that was a bad sign to begin with.

'Yes?' She had meant to start right in with her unsavoury little story, but there was something in his expression which made her wait for him to speak first.

He cleared his throat. 'Miss Kellaway, I've just had a very disturbing report from Joe Mellor.'

'That's odd,' said Jet, startled. 'You mean the security guard—he's the reason I wanted to speak to you.'

'Really? You surprise me. He's just been speaking to me about *you*.' Mr Allison's normally placid features looked grim and a little harried.

'What?' Jet pushed a lock of hair nervously behind her shoulder. 'Has he really? I honestly didn't think he'd dare.'

'Why wouldn't he? It may surprise you, Miss Kellaway, but a married man like Joe sometimes fails to appreciate young ladies who make passes—with or without glasses,' he tacked on humourlessly. 'He found your attempts to attract him most embarrassing.'

'What?' cried Jet again, as two angry dabs of colour rose prominently on her cheeks. 'Mr

Allison, Joe Mellor tried to assault me last night. I don't know what he's told you—I suppose that *I* enticed him—but that's just an attempt to squirm his way out of any consequences. Surely you don't believe him, do you?'

'I'm afraid I do, Miss Kellaway.' He picked up a pencil and drew a fat black line across his blotter. 'Yes, I'm afraid I do. Joe's been with us longer than you have, I've never had the slightest complaint about him before and he's performed his job entirely satisfactorily. You, on the other hand, had a very expensive effect on some of our equipment, and a very distracting effect on the staff in our sales department.'

Jet stared at him, her fists clenched tightly at her sides to prevent herself from pounding on his desk. And if he called her 'Miss Kellaway' in that tone just once more, she would scream.

But she didn't scream. Instead, with her eyes fixed steadily on his face, she told him how Joe had grabbed her as she was leaving, and kissed her.

'I told him I'd report him,' she explained, 'so I suppose he's just trying to put the blame on me.'

'Hmm. It's a good story, Miss Kellaway.' Mr Allison placed his elbows on the desk and pressed his fingertips carefully together. 'But I'm afraid I really can't buy it. Pretty girls like you always cry "sexual harrassment" when you need a way out of an awkward situation. It's happened twice before in this office.'

'And how do you know the men weren't guilty?' Jet's fists were clenched so hard now that her nails were biting into her palms.

'They weren't,' he replied succinctly.

'All right, even if they weren't, that doesn't mean I...'

'Miss Kellaway,' he sounded tired now, 'I put up with your disastrous effect on the office machinery, and even with the disruption of my sales staff since the men involved assured me it was not your fault. But this business last night is really more than I'm willing to tolerate. I'm not even particularly interested in who began it. I just need someone in your job who will not continually be the centre of a crisis.'

'Mr Allison...'

He held up his hand. 'I'm sorry, Miss Kellaway.' Just for a moment, he really did look sorry. 'But we won't be needing your services any longer.'

Jet opened her mouth to protest, but found herself shaking with such uncontrollable rage that she knew if she didn't get out of his office immediately she would throw everything in it at his head. Then he'd have a *genuine* cause for complaint. In any case, she had no wish to stay at Gourmet any longer. Not if Mr Allison couldn't take her word against Joe Mellor's, and obviously just wanted her out of his sight.

With her lips pressed tightly together, she raked him with one last scornful glare, and was pleased to see his eyes drop. Then she marched proudly out of his office with her head held high and her dark eyes still flashing angry sparks.

She was still shaking when she pushed open the door of her bedsit, and this time its dreariness assaulted her almost like a blow in the face. She had lost another job, a reasonably well-paying one this time, and she felt as if she were condemned to this depressing hole forever.

She sank down on the divan and pillowed her face in her hands, shutting out the damp-stained walls and the sparse but well-worn furniture.

Damn. It wasn't fair, of course, but when was life ever fair? And what could she do now? She didn't want her job back, not if Mr Allison could treat her like some bird-brained little siren who amused herself by leading men up the garden path. It was bad enough that he had thought she would be involved in the bets going on in Sales. But of course there *were* women who would think that stupidity was amusing, particularly when they knew that none of the hopefuls involved had any hope of winning. And Mr Allison *had* believed her in the end.

Jet took her hands away from her face and sat up. If he had believed her that time, why not now? And how dared he accuse her of harassing Joe when it had been precisely the other way around?

Slowly she dragged herself over to the kitchen to plug in the kettle for a much needed cup of coffee. Of course it was obvious really, wasn't it? Mr Allison hadn't necessarily believed Joe, but he was glad of the excuse to get rid of her. If he had dismissed her over the wager business, it would have looked like spite because she had turned down his invitation to dinner. But, because she had turned him down, she had become an embarrassment to him. The more she thought about it, the more sure she became that his offer had indeed been kindly meant. Only she had not taken it that way, and he had known it and felt foolish. She made him uncomfortable now, and Joe had provided the justification for getting rid of her.

But it wasn't fair, and nor was it right that Joe should get away with it.

Her shoulders slumped despondently, and she was just pouring herself coffee when the phone rang.

It was Midge, the relief receptionist.

'Hi, Jetta,' she chirped, in a high-pitched voice which was bursting with curiosity. 'What happened? Why did you and that security man both get sacked?'

'Joe, too?' muttered Jet. 'So I was right. He *did* believe me, and it *was* just an excuse.'

'What?' Midge sounded startled.

'Nothing,' said Jet quickly. 'And you'd better ask Mr Allison why I was sacked.'

Midge mumbled that she had just meant to show concern, and hung up the phone in a huff.

My eye, thought Jet irritably as she poured water into her cup. Morbid nosiness is all that call was about, Midge Bracken, and you know it.

Her musings were interrupted by the sound of Daisy's electric tin-opener vibrating against the wall. It was making a fearful noise and was obviously on its last legs. When Daisy started to open a second tin, Jet felt her nerves turn grindingly on edge. She glanced down and saw that she had just poured a cup of hot water with nothing in it. Sighing bad-temperedly, she was reaching into the cupboard for a jar when Daisy turned the tin-opener on for the third time.

Jet lifted her arm to bang furiously on the wall. Then it occurred to her that, as Daisy obviously had no classes this morning, she might as well discuss this latest setback with her friend. Daisy was a down-to-earth soul, and maybe her sound common sense would help to put things in perspective.

But when she pounded the wall and shouted at Daisy to come over, it was not her plump friend, but John who eventually appeared outside her door.

'Hi, John,' she said dismally. 'I thought you were Daisy.'

John grinned. 'Well, I hope you'll survive the disappointment. What's up, Jetta? You look as if you've been flattened by a truck.'

'No, by a rotten, scheming, lying, lecherous little creep called Joe Mellor. I'm afraid I've lost another job.'

'Oh,' said John, smoothing his fair hair and looking puzzled. 'But that's not a disaster, is it? You're always losing jobs.'

'Oh, don't rub it in,' groaned Jet. 'You see, this time I really thought it would work. I was taking Seth's advice and saving money for night school...'

'Who's Seth?' John interrupted. 'Surely our man-hating Jetta hasn't got herself a boyfriend at last?'

'Oh, stop it, John, I'm not in the mood,' wailed Jet miserably. 'And I'm not man-hating at all.' She sighed. 'But I dare say I soon would be if Seth Hagan were the man in my life.'

'Then isn't it just as well that I haven't the remotest inclination to be anything of the sort?' said a cool, deep voice from the doorway. And in front of Jet's stunned gaze the door which John had not properly closed swung open, and Seth's striking figure sauntered into the room.

As soon as she saw him, she knew with devastating, almost doomlike clarity just how very much she had missed him. And, as clear brown eyes met hers, she thought, just for a second, that she saw a reflection of the same instant knowledge in his. But it must have been an illusion, because he was staring at her with a coldness that was almost contempt, and the tightness in the muscles around his mouth belied any thought at all that he might care.

And, as this realisation came to her, another revelation, more devastating than the last, destroyed all the vows she had made years ago about guarding her heart from hurt. Her brittle protective shell shattered like brilliant shards of glass—and she saw that what she had been trying to resist without knowing it from the day she had met Seth had happened.

She had fallen in love with this tough, complex, sometimes intimidating—and incredibly sexy man. And it wasn't just a physical attraction. It was the thing which at the back of her mind she had always dreamed of.

But as she looked up at the beloved face before her, she knew from what she saw there that the dream already lay in ruins at her feet.

CHAPTER SIX

SETH studied Jet's slender figure. He had not seen her for over two months, and was surprised by the feeling of tenderness which very briefly assaulted him as he thought for a moment that she was actually trembling. He half stepped towards her, and at once she lifted her chin up and delivered an icy glare. Wrong again, he thought disgustedly, his protective instinct laid immediately to rest. This was no trembling maiden in distress, this was Jet Kellaway, Walking Liability, who had just cost him a long and valued client. The anger which had propelled him here in the first place took over.

'Who's this?' he snapped, jerking his head rudely in John's direction.

Jet's chin rose higher. 'This is my friend John, Mr Hagan,' she replied sweetly. 'John, this charming gentleman is Seth. As you can see, *not* my boyfriend.'

'Hi,' muttered John, extending a doubtful hand.

Seth glowered at him, conquered an unexpected and completely unjustifiable urge to bloody the young man's inoffensive nose and, after a long, simmering pause, extended his hand in return.

'Hello,' he responded, in a voice which came out like a snarl.

John looked thoroughly confused. 'Did you say this *wasn't* your boyfriend?' he asked sceptically.

'Does it look like it?'

'Well—to be honest—yes.' John glanced quickly at two startled, indignant faces, both of which looked ready to do him harm, and decided the atmosphere in this room was becoming too warm for him to handle. He also concluded that the man Jet called Seth was probably not homicidal, and with a murmured goodbye he beat a strategic retreat.

'Did you *have* to be so rude to him?' Jet asked nastily, moving quickly across the room to flop down on the divan.

As Seth started to come towards her, she jumped up again and exchanged her seat for the chair.

'Probably not,' he drawled. His eyes glinted unpleasantly as she crouched like a rabbit waiting to make a bolt. 'Did you *have* to lose me one of my best clients? I've had George Allison on my books since I took over the business from my father eight years ago. We've always got along with each other very well. A thoroughly successful partnership. Or it was, until you came along.' He put his hand to the bridge of his nose and held it there. 'I should have known better than to send you to Gourmet. Which is exactly what Marian said, of course.'

'Of course. Why *did* you send me there, then?' Jet tilted her nose haughtily and pretended she didn't care.

Seth lowered his hand, and the strained, harsh lines of his face seemed to soften for a moment and she couldn't read the look she saw in his eyes. 'I don't know,' he said, after a long silence. 'I honestly don't know, Jet.' He didn't sound angry now, only tired.

She stared at him, her hands pressed flat on the arms of her chair, and without being asked to he crossed the room and sat down on the divan.

'Make yourself comfortable,' muttered Jet sarcastically, because she didn't want him to know he had the power to hurt.

'I will.' Deliberately he swung his long legs off the floor and settled his shoulders against the headrest. As his eyes issued a challenge across the space between them, Jet felt a desperate longing to close that space, to lay herself down beside him and to rest her head on the place where his heart must be.

But his next words brought her up sharply and made her think he must have read her thoughts. She changed her mind about laying her head on his heart because she decided he probably didn't have one.

'Did you move there so I couldn't sit beside you?' he asked, in a voice which was intended to provoke.

'No,' replied Jet, untruthfully.

'Good. Then come and join me over here.'

'What for? Do you want me to pay my debts, too—like Joe Mellor? Not that I owe you anything.'

'Like hell you don't.' Suddenly Seth was on his feet, towering over her, and before she could open her mouth to scream for John he had pulled her up to face him. Both his hands were on her shoulders, and because there was only an inch of space between them she could feel the heat of his body warming hers.

'Don't,' she whispered, knowing she couldn't bear it if he kissed her now in anger.

'Don't worry,' he said scornfully, 'I won't.'

'Won't what?'

'Kiss you. Is that all you ever think of, butterfly? Kisses, causing trouble—and messing up my business. What in hell do you mean by saying you don't owe me anything?'

Jet swallowed hard. 'I—I *never* think of kisses. And I—didn't mean—I mean, of course I owe you something—a lot, but ...'

'But *what*?'

At the harshness of his tone, she felt what Daisy called her 'gumption' returning. His hands were still on her shoulders and she pushed them off forcefully—and then wished she didn't miss the feel of them through her blouse.

'But I don't owe you what Joe Mellor tried to take. And, Seth, it *wasn't* my fault.'

'It never is, is it?'

'But it wasn't. Joe kissed me. When I told him I'd report him, he told Mr Allison I'd tried to make advances to *him*. As if I would. Pig-eyed little creep.'

Seth's hands descended heavily on her shoulders again, and this time she didn't bother to push them away.

'George Allison doesn't buy that story, Jet. Tell me why *I* should?'

'Because it's true. And Mr Allison does believe it, because he's sacked Joe Mellor, too. Besides, Seth ...' Her eyes met his steadily. 'You know Joe. And what's more important, you know me. So you ought to know the truth.'

'Ought I? Yes, I know you all right. You remind me of——' He broke off abruptly.

'What do I remind you of, Seth?'

He shook his head. 'Who, not what. But it doesn't matter. The point is, I know what people like you can do to other people.'

'What do you mean? I'm not "people like me".
I'm Jet Kellaway. And—Seth, you *do* believe me,
don't you?'

Jet waited, and it was as if all her world de-
pended on his answer. She watched him and saw
the pain there, and a bitterness which had not been
so noticeable before.

'Does it matter so much that I believe you?' he
asked quietly, seeing something in her eyes which
he couldn't understand.

'Yes. Yes, it does.' There was no point in trying
to save her dignity by denying it. She could only
tell him how she felt.

Seth stared down at her, and she saw the hard
look in his eyes change to a puzzled bewilderment.
He shook his head, shrugged, and then replied as
though he couldn't understand himself, 'Yes. I'm
not at all sure why, but I do believe you, if it makes
a difference.' He frowned. 'In fact, now that I think
about it, I suspect George was looking for an excuse
to get rid of Hagan's. I expect he had an offer of
lower rates from another agency. He'd hardly have
cancelled us for one slip-up otherwise.' He smiled
wryly. 'Even if the slip-up was you.'

'But it wouldn't have been businesslike of you to
yell at Mr Allison, would it?' said Jet drily. 'So you
decided to yell at me instead. That's the real truth
of the matter, isn't it?'

'Hmm!' For a moment he looked surprised. Then
he nodded slowly and admitted she was probably
right. 'And I apologise for yelling,' he added
sheepishly. His smile was so boyishly penitent that
it made Jet want to pat him on the head and
murmur soothing endearments. But Seth wasn't the

sort of man you patted on the head, so she only smiled back and told him his apology was accepted.

Then her eyes grew very big as Seth's hand began to curve around her neck. His other hand lifted her chin towards his face as her eyes fastened on his lips so close to hers. They were as seductive and unavoidable as they had been since the moment she met him.

With a little cry she closed the space between them, put her arms around Seth's shoulders and with her fingers in his hair pulled his mouth eagerly down to hers. And she kissed him, not in payment of a debt, but because she loved him. He returned her kiss, gave her back as much as she had given, with such tenderness, passion and longing that Jet's tawdry little room became a palace, transformed for an instant by magic.

Seth's hands slid down her back, slowly, touching all the tender places she had thought would never again respond to a man's touch. Because she had not wanted to feel this way ever again. But now she did.

His lips explored her mouth, tasted its sweetness as she tasted him. And she felt the wonder of his male body against her own as for a few precious moments she thought that she had found her personal heaven at last.

Then his kiss became harder, desperate, as though it must last him for a lifetime, and, as she tried to hold him, with a stifled little groan he let her go.

'Seth?' she whispered, questioning, and now very much afraid. Of what, she wasn't even sure.

He turned away from her and his eyes seemed fixed on a cigarette burn in the faded rug which lay beside the divan. But when, after a long time, he

lifted his head to look at her, she realised that his
thoughts had been far from the dilapidated surroundings. His eyes seemed darker, more intense,
and there was a confused hunger in them that made
her want to cry.

'Seth, what is it?' she asked unhappily. 'What's
happened?'

He shook his head, ran a hand through his hair
and didn't answer. And it was then that it came to
her that something had felt different about him
when they kissed. Funny she hadn't noticed it when
he came in. But then, of course, she had been so
stunned to see him again...

'You've grown your hair!' she exclaimed without
thinking. Her mood changed abruptly from sadness
to satisfaction. 'I *knew* you'd look even more
hopelessly beautiful with it longer. And your
clothes... You're wearing a beige shirt instead of
a white one, and those heavenly dark brown
trousers...'

'Thanks,' said Seth dampeningly, the confused
look rapidly fading from his eyes as well. 'I'm glad
you approve. But if you call me "beautiful" again,
young woman, I promise you I'll break your pretty
arm.'

Jet giggled as the tension drained out of her. 'All
right. Handsome, then. But you're not really
handsome, are you?'

Seth raised his eyes to the ceiling. 'I wouldn't
know. Shall we change this fascinating subject and
start discussing you, instead? You're looking much
better. Lovely as ever, but no longer a starving
swan.'

Jet smiled. He had called her lovely. 'Well, since
we both approve of each other's appearance...' she

began laughingly. Then the laughter died in her throat as he interrupted her.

'Yes, but Marian doesn't approve of the change in me at all.' His tone was flat, and she wondered if he had meant to hurt her, to burst the bubble of hope he had seen glowing in her eyes. But of course he had to burst it, she knew that. He was going to be married soon. He had returned her kiss, but it meant nothing. What normal, self-centred man would pass up what was handed to him so eagerly—so *stupidly*—by a reasonably pretty woman who wasn't too thin and hungry any more?

Men. Self-centred, self-seeking, arrogant. Of course they were all the same. Like Gino. Like Seth. She had only herself to blame if she had let herself get hurt.

By now she wasn't sure if her anger was directed at Seth or at herself, but she was angry with someone and Seth was a handy target—lounging there against the door of her cupboard as if he owned it—*and*, she noticed, searching for a cigarette. In *her* home. Which contained no ashtrays. It was dingy and depressing enough here as it was, without adding the smell of stale tobacco.

As Seth pulled the packet from his pocket, the hurt and unhappiness which had been growing in her exploded.

'What do you think you're doing?' she shouted. 'This is *my* house. And you're not stinking it up with your rotten cigarette.'

Seth paused with a cigarette half-way to his lips— which curved in a faint sneer as, very slowly, very deliberately, he pulled the packet out again, replaced the cigarette, and returned it carefully to his pocket. And all the time his wide-set eyes were fastened derisively on her face.

'Satisfied?' he asked acidly, when the operation was completed.

'Yes,' spat Jet, her dark hair rippling forward over her shoulder. 'I am. I should have thought your Marian would be, too. She strikes me as the sort of woman who if she found a cat hair in her house would wash it and hang it out to dry. Does she actually let you *smoke*?'

Seth smiled, a sensuous, arousing and deliberately taunting smile. 'I do what I choose to do, butterfly. But as a matter of fact Marian is a very— accommodating—woman.'

Jet had a sudden vision of Marian with her blonde hair down, 'accommodating' Seth, and she felt something black and painful curl up in her stomach.

'Is she really?' she jeered, her emotions now totally out of control. 'How lucky for you. But in that case, the only thing I don't understand is why you're bothering to marry her.'

That touched him, more than she had expected. The full lips twisted angrily, and for a moment his face went very white and cold. Then his normal colour returned and he replied cuttingly, 'Because, my dear, unlike you, when I make a commitment I honour it.'

'Really. How pompous. And I suppose you think kissing me isn't breaking that commitment?'

That touched him, too. She saw him ram his hands forcefully into his pockets as if he were afraid that if he left them loose he might be tempted to hit her. 'No,' he said tightly. 'No, I don't think that. On the other hand, as your favours are so easily given, perhaps Marian doesn't have much to worry about. You're hardly a serious threat.'

At that, Jet's hurt and anger erupted completely. Had she actually convinced herself she *loved* this man?

In the end it wasn't Seth who hit Jet, but the other way around. With a sound like air bursting from a tyre, she flung herself across the room, raised her hand and slapped him—hard—across the face.

He didn't move. Instead he stood absolutely still, his face expressionless—and flaming red where she had struck him. Jet faced him, expecting retaliation which never came.

'Well?' she cried, when she could stand it no longer. 'Aren't you going to say anything?'

'I think I've said enough already.'

'Yes,' said Jet, all of a sudden deadeningly deflated. 'You have, haven't you. Did you mean it?'

'I expect so, at the time.' His voice was incredibly weary now and, her anger evaporated, Jet wanted desperately to give comfort. But instead she stepped backwards and asked cautiously, 'But you don't mean what you said any more?'

'I don't know what I mean any more. I can't even think straight when you're around, butterfly. But one thing I *am* certain of...' his jaw tightened 'is that I can't stand the idea of Joe Mellor mauling you about.'

'I couldn't stand it either, and it was *not* my idea, if that's what you're trying to imply. Anyway, I don't see why you should care.'

'Neither do I.'

And he didn't. Not for the first time since meeting Jet, he thought he must be going mad. It was time he got out of this house, out of Jet's life and back to the soothing, sensible arms of his fiancée. And that worm of an idea, somewhere at the back of his mind, that he didn't much want to be soothed, could go take a jump in Lost Lagoon.

'Look,' he said quietly, 'I'm sorry. Sorry I came barging over here to upset you when you must have been upset already, sorry I made those very un-called-for remarks about your character...'

'And I'm sorry I hit you. Very sorry. Are—are you also sorry you kissed me?' She wondered why her palms were suddenly damp.

Seth stared at her, and she saw various shades of feeling cross his face, none of which she could interpret at all clearly. Finally he brushed an arm across his forehead, which was glistening with perspiration, and said blankly, 'No. I don't believe I am. Although strictly speaking, it was you who kissed me.'

'Not the first time.'

'True.' He hesitated. 'Jet, I ... I truly regret ... No. Let's start again. You and I—it's been—an experience. A remarkably stimulating experience at times,' he added with a brief attempt at humour. 'But I'm committed to Marian, as you so rightly pointed out. She suits me. And she'll have good reason to be angry if I find you yet another job. So I'm afraid you're on your own, butterfly. Do you think you can manage?'

'I've always managed,' said Jet dully, not looking at him. 'How do you think I coped before you came along?'

'Not very well,' he replied flatly, gesturing at the dreary surroundings.

'Well enough.'

'I suppose so.' He paused, started to reach for a cigarette, and then stopped with a half-guilty grin on his face. 'Right. You can cope. But you know what I think?'

'What?' She didn't really care what he thought, because he was going to leave her.

'I think you should stop all this job nonsense. It just doesn't seem to work for you, does it? Find some nice man who'll be crazy enough to marry you. Then he can work, and you can raise a brood of beautiful children. That's what you said you wanted, wasn't it? Work with children?'

'I said I wanted to *teach* children, you chauvinistic, patronising, ego-tripping idiot.' She knew there was a break in her voice, and that at any moment she was going to say more than she should. But she felt as if everything that mattered was being taken away from her, and she couldn't halt the words that came pouring out of her mouth.

'Yes, I do want children. Lots of them. But I'll never have them, Seth Hagan.'

'I don't see...'

'No, you wouldn't see, would you? Everything's always gone right for you, just the way you planned it. Education, work, girlfriends, marriage to an equally well-ordered woman—but that's not the way it's been for me, Seth. Oh, yes, I planned to have children. And when I got pregnant I was the happiest girl in the world—in spite of the circumstances. But then I lost my baby and they said I'd probably never have another. So you see, your neat little scenario for me just isn't going to happen. And there aren't too many men around who want a woman who can't have children. Not to marry, that is.'

She paused for breath, and saw that Seth was frowning at her. Had he even understood what she had told him?

'*You* had a baby?'

So he understand that much at least. 'Yes. I had a baby. That's what I said.'

'So I was right.'

Jet gaped at him. 'Right about what?' And then, as he continued to scowl at her, she understood. He thought she hadn't been married to Gino, and that, in his very proper books, made her a 'fallen woman'. Well, to hell with him. He wanted to get out of her life, and he could get out. Now.

'Yes, Seth,' she said, very clearly and coldly. 'You were right. And now you can go and play judge and jury somewhere else. With Marian. She'll love it.' Lifting both her hands, she grabbed him by one arm and towed him, unresisting, towards the door.

When she opened it and tried to push him through, he stopped and started to say something. But she cut him off, and with an almighty shove in the back sent him catapulting down the step. And she knew he hadn't tried to stop her because he really wanted to go.

Just as she was closing the door, she saw him lift his head to look at her. His face was very still and it looked grim and unrelenting—and suddenly much older. And then she closed the door, shutting him out. But it was several minutes later before she heard his car start up and take off, surprisingly slowly, down the road.

Jet returned to the divan, buried her face in the cushion, and didn't lift it again until she heard Daisy laughing when she returned home from college late in the afternoon.

*　　*　　*

I'll never see Seth again. The words kept going round and round in her head as she stumbled about the kitchen three days later, trying to find her jar of instant coffee. Then she remembered there wasn't any, because she and John and Daisy had finished the last of it the night before. Damn. Eleven o'clock in the morning and she had no coffee. That was all she needed. From the silence next door she knew there was no hope there either, which meant she would have to go to Mr Cheung's.

She had not been outside at all since the day Seth had walked—or been pushed—out of her door. A cheque had come from Mr Allison, so there was no need to worry about money, and somehow she hadn't felt up to facing the world again just yet—not even nice old Mr Cheung at the corner store. But John and Daisy, concerned about her, had been over several times to stir her out of her apathy, and she knew from past experience that it wouldn't be long before she picked up the pieces of her life and carried on as she had always done. After all, she was no worse off than she had been before she met Seth. Was she?

Seth. She slammed the kitchen cupboard shut and wandered over to inspect her wardrobe. Obviously she couldn't go out in her sadly ancient pink nightie with the kangaroo on the front. Seth. Why *had* she told him about the baby? It was something she hadn't wanted him to know, not only because there was no point in telling him, but also because it was something she tried not to think about herself. Even after seven years the pain was still there—and the emptiness. The little boy who had never had a name had only been growing in her for four months when she'd lost him, but she still felt a part of her had been cruelly torn away. And by that time she had already lost Gino, so there had been nobody left for her to love. Until Seth. As soon as she found him, and knew that she loved him, he too had vanished from her life.

As she groped at the back of the cupboard for a pair of clean slacks, she wondered for the hundredth time why Seth was the way he was. So judgemental and severe most of the time, seeming utterly detached and controlled. And yet he had grown his hair, and he had a smile that could melt her blood, and sometimes—rarely—he became the warm, laughing and very sexy man she knew she loved.

Jet tugged on black slacks. They weren't particularly clean, after all, but she decided she didn't care. What had Seth meant when he said she reminded him of someone else? Someone who did things to other people. She should have asked him, she supposed, but at the time it hadn't seemed important. Well, whoever that someone was, Jet thought she had a lot to answer for.

She was just reaching for a blouse when there was a sharp rap on the door. Hastily pulling on the nearest garment, which happened to be a paint-stained shirt she did her housework in, she fastened the buttons without looking what she was doing, and went to admit Daisy or John. With any luck, they might be bearing coffee.

Only it wasn't either Daisy or John who stood on the shallow step staring up at her. It was Marian. And all she had with her was a handbag. Although, when her eyes fell on Jet's dishevelled appearance, she produced a chillingly supercilious smile.

CHAPTER SEVEN

'GOOD morning, Miss Flyaway.' Marian's voice was as chilling as her smile.

'Kellaway,' said Jet automatically, and knowing as soon as the words were out of her mouth that she had risen like a plump, silly salmon to the bait.

'Of course. May I come in, Miss—Kellaway?' She already had one shapely foot through the door, and Jet, still catatonic with surprise, fell back as Marian swept into the room, her smart grey suit and expensive shoes looking ridiculously out of place in Jet's small and shabby home. Her cool blue eyes ran scathingly over the damp stains and came to rest on the only comfortable chair. 'May I sit down?'

Jet nodded, not knowing what else to do, although now that the first shock was over she was beginning to feel strong stirrings of indignation at this uninvited invasion of her totally inadequate territory. And she wished she wasn't wearing dusty black slacks and a shirt which had seen better days.

Marian sank gracefully on to the old tweed chair and crossed one elegant leg over the other. Jet, feeling she was at a sufficient disadvantage already, remained standing. 'Why are you here, Miss Sinclair?' she asked baldly.

Marian raised her perfectly plucked eyebrows. 'I came to talk to you, Miss . . .?'

'Kellaway,' said Jet through gritted teeth.

'Ah, yes. Miss Kellaway.' She waited for Jet to respond and, when she didn't, went on crisply, 'I understand you've been seeing something of Mr Hagan.'

'He was here three days ago, yes,' said Jet briefly, her eyes fixed carefully on the light switch to make sure she gave nothing away. She had no intention of telling this cucumber-cool lady that when she parted from Seth it had not been on friendly terms.

'Yes. I thought so.'

'Didn't he tell you?' Jet was vaguely surprised. Somehow she had thought that because of the fiasco with Mr Allison he would have mentioned their meeting. She had expected him to tell Marian that he had seen Miss Kellaway, but only to inform her that she would be getting no further employment through Hagan's.

'He may have said something,' replied Marian evasively.

Jet waited for her to go on. She wasn't going to give this patronising woman the satisfaction of appearing curious about her visit—which she hoped would end very soon.

Marian stretched a trim ankle and studied the toe of her shoe. Then she lifted her head quickly to look Jet straight in the eye. 'Miss Kellaway,' she began levelly, 'I've noticed a considerable change in my fiancé lately, and I don't think it's for the better.'

'Really?' said Jet faintly.

'Really. And I think the reason for the change is you.'

Indignation overcame Jet's curiosity to know what Marian was getting at, and she said sharply, 'Miss Sinclair, I didn't invite you here, I certainly don't want you here, and if you're having problems with Seth I suggest you had better sort them out with him.'

'So he's "Seth" to you now, is he?'

'He has been for some time,' said Jet, enjoying the opportunity to hit back.

'I suspected as much. That deplorable long hair, those *juvenile* clothes, and his attitude lately, which has really been quite incomprehensible. I *knew* this dreadful decline in his standards could only be laid at your door.'

Jet gave a short laugh and thumped down on the divan, no longer feeling at a disadvantage. 'The decline and fall of Miss Sinclair's perfect partner,' she said lightly. 'I think he's much nicer with a heart.' Then, seeing Marian's suddenly stricken face, she felt guilty. Perhaps this woman really did love Seth as much as she loved him herself. And Marian was the one Seth wanted. The one he said 'suited' him. And if Marian was right, and it was because of her that things had gone wrong between them, the least she could do for Seth was try to put them right.

'Look,' she said quickly, 'I *haven't* been seeing Seth. He gave me dinner once two months or so ago because he thought I looked hungry, and he came over here the other day to give me hell for losing him a client. I haven't *tried* to change him, and if he has changed at all, don't you think it might be an improvement? His clothes aren't juvenile at all. They're youthful and stylish.' She sighed. 'And they make him look quite devastatingly attractive. But he's going to marry *you*, Miss Sinclair, not me. He says you're right for him. I'm sure he knows his own mind, and it's your influence that will count with him in the end.'

Yes, she thought sadly. How true. A month from now Seth would be dressed in sober grey and white again and his hair would be short back and sides.

She looked up and saw that Marian was watching her with an expression of dawning—no, calculating—relief. 'Yes,' she said thoughtfully. 'Perhaps you're right.' She patted her neatly groomed hair. 'But I could have sworn...' She paused.

'What could you have sworn, Miss Sinclair?'

'I'm not sure. But for the last few months Seth *has* been behaving differently. It's not just his clothes. He's been less predictable, more—temperamental.' She shuddered slightly. 'And once or twice he's really been extremely rude. He always apologised afterwards, of course, and said he didn't know what had come over him. I'm not sure why, and he certainly never said so, but somehow I thought that this—this...'

'Deplorable decline?' suggested Jet with a certain malice.

Marian gave her an oblique look and nodded. 'Precisely. The point is, I thought it was your doing, and I came over here today to—ah—persuade you to leave him alone.'

Jet shook her head. 'I'd never want to hurt Seth, Miss Sinclair. He wants *you*. And you don't have to worry, you know, because I'm sure he won't come here again.'

Marian nodded, looking faintly puzzled, and the look she gave Jet was more wary now than hostile. 'I'll have to take your word for it, then, won't I?' she remarked, all cool and curt again. She uncrossed her legs and rose languidly to her feet. 'I'm sorry if I've disturbed you, Miss Kellaway. Thank you for your time. No, it's quite all right, don't bother to see me out.' With a final glance of distaste around Jet's lodgings, she crossed over to the door and disappeared.

Jet, who had started up to follow her, sagged wearily back against the wall. She felt exhausted already, and it was still only the middle of the day. She smiled wryly. If that abortive little interview had accomplishing nothing else, at least she had finally convinced Marian to call her 'Kellaway'.

She turned back to the cupboard and removed her handbag. A few minutes later she was walking through the bright July sunlight to Mr Cheung's. Though her heart felt like a black lump of coal and her legs seemed leaden weights, she still had to have coffee. But, glancing up at the white clouds chasing each other across the sapphire blue sky, irrationally she wished it would rain.

A week later Jet's wish had come true with a vengeance, and as she scurried down the street from the bus stop, hoping to reach her door before she was well and truly drenched, she berated herself for having even thought of rain.

The day after Marian's visit she had known it was time she pulled herself together, so she got dressed in what Seth had told her were suitable interview clothes, and sallied forth in search of a job. She had continued to sally all week because there was still money in the bank and she hadn't totally given up hope of saving more. Enough to go to college. After all, Seth had once said he had faith in her. But of course that had been before Joe and Mr Allison—before he had told her she should find someone crazy enough to marry her. Now she wasn't sure college really mattered.

Jet bent her head against a gust of wind and scowled down at the wet pavement. A large drop of rain slithered clammily down her neck, and with a shudder of discomfort she increased her pace so that by the time she reached her front door she was almost running. Which was why she didn't see the bulky figure looming in front of it until she tried to put her key in a lock which had turned unaccountably into the buttonhole of a man's damp tan-coloured blazer.

Now wait a minute... As her eyes rose slowly from the buttonhole to a smart chocolate brown tie knotted around a very familiar neck, Jet felt her arms and legs grow even colder—if that were possible. But a moment later her whole body was suffused with heat.

'Seth,' she murmured stupidly, her key poised uselessly in the air. 'Seth...'

'Yes, it's me. Do you think you can bear to let me in before we both perish from the cold—or drown in this less than romantic summer storm?'

'Like Tom and Maggie. In *The Mill on the Floss*,' murmured Jet vaguely, and not moving an inch. Then, as Seth stared down at her in disbelief, she quoted with dreamy irrelevance, '"In their death they were not divided."'

'Good heavens!' exclaimed Seth. 'You've got water on your brain for sure this time, butterfly. No. Not like Tom and Maggie at all. For one thing I am *not* your brother, thank goodness.' As she continued to stand there blankly, he removed the key from her fingers and inserted it decisively in the lock.

A minute later they were inside and Seth was shutting the door purposefully behind them.

Jet stared at him. His dark brown trousers were damp like the rest of him, and they clung to his firm thighs like a wet, sensuous glove. His shirt clung too. It was a rich cream colour and she could see the taut muscles outlined beneath the cloth. She passed her tongue slowly over her lips. 'What...why are you here?' she whispered.

'I wanted to see you again.' His voice was very deep and the greenish-brown eyes which she had once thought gentle had her in a dangerous hypnotic hold.

'Why?' She still couldn't get her voice above a whisper.

A drop trickled down Seth's forehead from the dark hair plastered to his head, and he pulled out a handkerchief to wipe it quickly across his face. 'Because I wanted to apologise for what I said to you.'

'What you said? But you didn't say anything when I—when I told you about the baby.'

To Jet's surprise, he moved his head impatiently, dismissing the subject which she had been sure must be uppermost in his mind. 'You didn't give me a chance, did you? But that's not what I'm talking about.'

'It's not?' Jet was utterly bewildered.

'No. I want to apologise for suggesting that all you were good for was marriage...'

'To a man crazy enough to have me,' Jet reminded him with an acid note in her voice.

He smiled ruefully. 'Did I really say that? You were right to call me a chauvinistic idiot.'

'Did I call you that?'

'As well as ego-tripping and patronising.' He smiled and took a step towards her, cupping her chin in the fingers of one hand while he scrutinised her face. 'You look like a drowned rat,' he announced, after several long, tense seconds during which Jet found it hard not to tremble. The touch of his hand was as intoxicating as it had always been.

She took a deep breath and moved her head away. 'That's not very original,' she remarked caustically, smoothing her skirt carefully over her hips—until she saw that he was following the movement of her hands with appreciation.

'Very nice,' he murmured approvingly. 'And I'm unoriginal, am I? Well, I suppose I could have said you look like a drowned gazelle. But you don't, really. At the moment rat's much more apt.'

'Thanks. You look pretty ratty yourself,' taunted Jet, thinking that in fact he looked irresistible.

'Don't mention it. And since we're both drowned...' His eyes gleamed suggestively. 'Perhaps I can propose a solution.'

'And if you're going to suggest we take everything off and have a hot bath, perhaps you can't.'

'The thought never crossed my mind,' said Seth virtuously, raising his eyes to the ceiling.

'I'm glad to hear it, because I was going to suggest that since you've made the apology you came to make, you'd better take yourself home and get into some warm clothes.' It wasn't what she wanted to say, but she didn't think she could trust herself around Seth much longer. At any moment she would find herself flinging her arms around his very wet neck.

But, instead of leaving, Seth only smiled and moved determinedly towards her. 'I'm not going anywhere, butterfly. And you're much too wet to fly away.'

He was standing right beside her now, and before she could move he had reached out a long arm and was peeling her sopping wet cardigan from her back. 'Don't you own an umbrella?' he asked softly.

'I used to. It broke. Don't you?' He was starting to unbutton her blouse now in a very businesslike fashion, and while she told herself she wanted to move away from him, her feet seemed to be glued helplessly to the floor.

'I used to too, in my student days. But since I've worked downtown, with my car in the underground car park, I haven't needed one. Until tonight.' With calm efficiency he peeled her blouse off and it followed the cardigan on to the floor.

'Now kick those wet shoes off,' he directed.

Mesmerised, Jet did as she was told, and found herself standing before him in nothing but a well-mended slip, a very damp skirt and tights. Her scattered wits began slowly to return. 'You didn't need an umbrella tonight either,' she pointed out. 'You could have waited in your car.'

'And have you slip by me and slam the door in my face?'

'I wouldn't have.'

'Wouldn't you?' His tone was enigmatic, and as his gaze travelled rather sternly over her body, she shivered.

Immediately Seth moved into action. 'You're cold,' he said accusingly. 'Here.' Without a by your leave he pulled open her clothes cupboard, grabbed the first garment he saw, which happened to be her old paint-stained shirt, and told her to put it on. 'Then go and have a bath while I wait for you,' he ordered. 'After that, you can put on something warm and...' he eyed the stained shirt with revulsion, 'something *clean*. I'm going to take you home for dinner.'

Jet, who was now grovelling in her cupboard for a dry skirt and top, cast him a scathing look over her shoulder. 'Am I the main course?' she asked flippantly. And then, when she saw the threatening look in his eye, 'All right, I'll have a bath and get dressed. But if you hang around in that wet jacket and shirt much longer you're going to catch pneumonia. I'm *not* having dinner with you, Seth, so I think you'd better go away.'

'I'm *not* going away without you.' There was such warmth in his voice and his lips slanted so seductively that, before she realised what she was doing, Jet had trotted obediently into her tiny bathroom and was turning on the taps. Then she poked her head round the door again, saw him still standing in the middle of the room looking very wet and alluring, and told him to take his jacket off and sit down.

He grinned at her. 'I daren't. Unless you want to start growing mushrooms in your chair. As you've already observed, I'm still exceedingly wet. Now, for pity's sake, stop arguing and hurry up.'

Jet hurried up, and a few minutes later emerged from the bathroom in a pale blue robe, and told Seth to turn his back. 'It's impossible to move in there,' she explained briefly, feeling unaccountably embarrassed.

As soon as she had on her skirt—the red flowered one again—and had dragged a soft black sweater over the top of her head, Jet felt she could face Seth on her own terms and told him to turn around.

'There. Now, will you please go away, Seth? You know I can't have dinner with you.'

'You were wearing that skirt the first time I saw you,' he murmured irrelevantly. '*Why* can't you?'

'Because of Marian.' There. It was out in the open. The cool and collected presence of the cucumber lady which had been haunting them since the moment they stepped through the door.

'Oh, yes. Marian.' Seth's eyes were unnervingly still.

Jet, whose emotions were already stretched almost to breaking point, felt them stretch even further. 'What do you mean, "Oh, yes, Marian"? Seth, you can't just forget about her when it suits you.'

'I haven't forgotten about her. She's part of the reason I'm here.'

'That doesn't make any sense, and you know it.' Jet couldn't take much more of this game he seemed to be playing.

'It does, as a matter of fact. You see, Marian hasn't been at all pleased with me lately. She says I've changed for the worse. She doesn't like my hair or my clothes or my attitude.' He grinned. 'Whereas I'm rather enjoying them myself. The result was that we had...' He hesitated.

'Did you have a blazing argument?' prompted Jet, not quite wanting to hope.

'Not exactly. We had a very civilised disagreement, during which Marian told me she had been to see you, and that although she didn't think you had set out to undermine my hitherto sterling character, regrettably that was what had happened. I told her she was talking rubbish, and she said if I had any sense left at all, which she doubted, I'd think about what she was saying very seriously. After which, I suppose, I was expected to come to my senses and agree that of course she was absolutely right.'

'And did you?'

'No. I came to see you instead.'

'Well, now you've seen me,' said Jet in exasperation. 'And as you're still engaged to Marian I think you had better take yourself off.' There was a slight break in her voice as she added, 'I don't want to interfere with your happiness, Seth. Go and make your peace with Marian.'

Seth lifted his hand and absently curled a lock of her long, damp hair around his fingers. 'You're really a very nice girl, aren't you, butterfly?' he murmured. 'I don't think I realised just how nice you were before.'

'Seth, please...' Jet's eyes were dark and filled with pain. 'Please don't...'

'Don't what? I don't want to hurt you, little butterfly. Coming to my house for a meal won't be so very awful, will it?' He was surprised to realise how much her answer mattered.

'It's not that. But you're still going to marry Marian. It wouldn't be fair to her...'

'Oh. Is that it?' His fingers tightened involuntarily in her hair. 'I guess I didn't explain it properly, did I? Marian has postponed the wedding—indefinitely. She says she doesn't want to see me for two months. During that time we're both to see other people if we want to. After that we'll decide whether to go ahead with the marriage.'

'But—she's your secretary,' protested Jet, fastening on the aspect that mattered least because she couldn't grasp the rest of it right away.

'That's hardly a problem in my line of work,' he replied impatiently. 'I've found her work somewhere else and Mary's taking over her job until I find someone permanent.'

'Oh. Yes, I see.'

'Do you? Good. Then can we please bring this absorbing discussion of my business to an end, so I can get home and change out of these wet clothes?'

Hastily Jet squelched a mouth-watering vision of Seth removing his sodden shirt and trousers. She had no idea how he really felt about the temporary break-up with Marian. In fact, she had a feeling he didn't know himself. But that was no reason for her to make an already confused situation any worse.

'We can certainly end this conversation,' she said resolutely. 'You're leaving immediately and I'm staying. Goodbye, Seth.'

It took all her strength to say it, and she might as well have saved her breath. Because Seth, muttering some graphic but well-chosen phrases, suddenly released her hair, put both hands on her waist and hoisted her with irritating ease across his shoulder.

Jet was too surprised to resist, and when Seth reached the door it occurred to him that he was just as surprised himself. With another muttered curse he put her down.

They stared at each other, their eyes very bright and both of them breathing hard. Then suddenly Jet started to smile.

'Tarzan or Rambo?' she asked mischievously, in a voice that was not quite steady.

Seth eyed her doubtfully, and then he began to smile too. 'King Kong, I expect,' he said cheerfully, 'and we all know where his antics got him.'

Jet laughed, and in a moment they were both laughing as if he had just made the funniest comment in the world.

'Go get a coat or something, Jet,' said Seth presently, when both of them had laughed themselves to exhaustion.

Jet gave up trying to resist him and went to do as he asked.

When they got outside it had stopped raining.

'You've got a new car!' she exclaimed, when they reached the street, and she saw a neat little gold-coloured Corvette parked beside the kerb.

'Mm. Like it? Marian doesn't.'

'But it's gorgeous,' cried Jet enthusiastically. Then she thought a moment and added, 'But of course it does rather change your image.'

'Does it, now?' murmured Seth non-committally as they pulled away from the kerb. 'And how do you figure that?'

Jet grinned. 'You know. From staid and stuffy businessman to sporty young executive hunk.'

Seth lunged at her, then realised he was aiming the car straight for her neighbour's tiny hedge.

'You'll pay for that remark, young lady,' he assured her, as he swung the Corvette back to its side of the road.

'I can hardly wait,' teased Jet, causing him to swerve sideways at an unsuspecting fence.

'You won't have to if you keep that up,' he remarked drily. 'We'll both be upside-down in a ditch.'

But as it turned out they arrived at the house in West Vancouver without further incident, because Jet stopped baiting Seth and settled down to enjoy the drive with him over the rain-slicked streets. The evening sun was beaming a watery light at last, and the tops of the mountains gleamed golden above pink trailing clouds.

Somehow Jet had expected that Seth's home would be old and dark and Victorian, set well back from the road at the end of a long, quiet lane. In fact, it was light and spacious and modern. Situated at the end of a very short turning off the Upper Levels Highway, it was built of natural cedar which blended perfectly with the rocky hillside on which it perched. In front of the house stretched a magnificent view of the waters of Burrard Inlet just now beginning to reflect the lights of small boats as they lit up for the evening, while across the inlet loomed the wooded acres of Stanley Park.

Jet jumped out of the car and stood spellbound. 'It's beautiful,' she breathed, as her eyes roamed from the stunning view to the spectacular house, and back again. 'Is it really all yours? I mean, do you live here by yourself?'

Seth raised his eyebrows in that way that made her stomach curl. 'Why? Do you suspect me of harbouring a secret harem in the attic?'

Jet laughed. 'No, not really. But it's such a huge place for one person.'

'Ah, but I think ahead, you see. I had this built when I took over Hagan's eight years ago. I never intended to spend the rest of my life alone. Contrary to your peculiar conceptions about me, I *do* have quite normal inclinations. I want a wife and family one day just like anyone else.'

'Yes, I know about the wife part,' replied Jet with unnecessary tartness.

'Of course you do,' agreed Seth, taking her authoritatively by the arm. 'Come along, then. Let's see if you're as enthusiastic about the inside of my home. And I want to introduce you to my father and Mrs Crabtree.'

'Your father?' said Jet faintly. 'But I thought you said you lived alone.'

'I used to. But Dad moved in with me when mother finally—left. And Mrs Crabtree, who isn't at all like her name, looks after the two of us.'

'Do you need looking after?' Jet was genuinely surprised. It had never occurred to her that the self-sufficient Seth Hagan might actually depend on someone else.

'Of course. Doesn't everybody sometimes?'

'No,' said Jet flatly, 'I don't.'

Seth's fingers curled around her arm. 'That's the biggest piece of nonsense I've heard in a very long time.'

Jet tossed her head. 'It's *not* nonsense...' she began.

But Seth was paying no attention. Instead he was steering her inexorably towards the high front doors. As he turned the key Jet tried to hang back, feeling a sudden inexplicable shyness at the thought of meeting Seth's father. But his arm was firmly around her waist now, which left her no chance to escape.

The entrance to Seth's house was as impressive as the outside. At the back of a large, airy front hall which was lit by a softly tinted skylight, a flight of stairs curved up to a gallery which circled around behind them. And at the top of the stairs stood a small, white-haired man wearing dark, thick glasses and an exceptionally sweet smile. His face lit up when he saw Seth and his companion, and he came hurrying down the stairs to greet them. Fleetingly, Jet thought that he was remarkably spry for such a frail-looking man. Then she didn't think of anything except the wonderful warmth of his welcome.

'You must be Seth's butterfly,' he beamed, taking her hand in a surprisingly firm grip. 'He phoned to tell me you were coming, and I can only say I'm delighted.'

Jet glanced sideways at Seth. So he had been so sure of her, he had told his father she was coming, had he? She would have a bone to pick with him about that later. But for now all she wanted to do was bask in this charming old man's obvious delight in her company.

'Thank you,' she murmured shyly. She paused. 'Did Seth really call me his—his...'

'Butterfly? Yes, he did, and I must say after Miss Sinclair the news was a great relief.'

'Dad doesn't much care for Marian,' explained Seth, poker-faced.

'Oh, but I'm not—I mean... Oh, dear.'

'What Jet is trying to tell you, Dad,' said Seth, still looking stony, 'is that she is not in any way a replacement for Marian. She puts up with me on occasions, but she thinks I'm arrogant and self-satisfied—and dull.'

'Don't blame her,' grunted Hagan senior, before Jet could refute Seth's statement. 'I'm Roger Hagan, by the way, since my son doesn't seem inclined to introduce us.'

'You didn't give me a chance, Dad,' objected Seth. His voice was resigned, but his eyes were full of affection.

'Don't suppose I did. Well, well. Come and sit down, my dear.' He took Jet's arm courteously and led her to a small, comfortable den just off the main hall, while Seth went to change his clothes.

'This is where we usually sit,' he explained. 'The living-room is really too big for just Seth and me, and Mrs Crabtree always goes home after dinner. Don't you, Mrs Crabtree?' He turned to a tall, svelte redhead who had just swayed into the room—and who certainly did belie her unfortunate name.

Jet's instant and unreasonable pang of what she was very much afraid must be jealousy was assuaged immediately when Mrs Crabtree snorted and replied brusquely that she should think she did, because she'd had quite enough of the two of them by the end of the day, and in any case her husband came off evening shift at ten o'clock.

Roger Hagan chuckled. 'Ah, you know you'd be lost without us, Mrs Crabtree,' he told her with a twinkle in his eye.

Mrs Crabtree returned the chuckle. 'Not as lost as you'd be,' she retorted.

'True,' murmured Seth as he strolled in, looking devastatingly glamorous in dark trousers and a wine-coloured jacket. 'What are we having for dinner?'

'See what I mean?' The redhead shot a triumphant glance at Jet, who grinned and said she saw all too clearly.

'You can't cook, then?' she asked, trying to keep her mind off the way Seth's trousers hugged his thighs as he bent over a tray of drinks.

'Not so you'd notice,' he replied, handing her a glass of something pink and bubbly.

Jet stared at it. 'What on earth is this?' she asked, laughing.

'You may well ask,' replied Roger Hagan drily. 'Whatever it is, it's Miss Sinclair's favourite drink.'

Jet stopped laughing abruptly and Seth cleared his throat. 'Sorry,' he muttered, looking ridiculously embarrassed. 'Habit.'

'No problem, it's very good,' replied Jet sipping stoically. There was no way she was going to let Seth know she was hurting. Besides, the odd-looking concoction *was* good, and she might just as well enjoy it. She took another sip and felt its warmth seep slowly through her body.

A few minutes later Mrs Crabtree summoned them to the dining room to eat.

During the meal, a beautifully cooked casserole of lamb and vegetables, they chatted generally about the weather, Seth's house and how his business was going. He asked Jet if she had found another job yet, and she said, yes, she was starting at a flower shop in a month. It wasn't strictly true but, just because Marian had departed from the scene, she didn't want Seth to think he was obliged to employ her once more. She couldn't bear it if something went wrong yet again, and the florist had *almost* promised to take her on. She was going to let her know for sure next week.

After dinner the three of them retired to the den with coffee, and half an hour after that Roger said he was retiring to his bed.

'He's nice, isn't he?' smiled Jet as he left the room.

'Yes,' agreed Seth, looking fondly after his father. 'And you must have made a hit. He never left the room before midnight when Marian came over here. Figured I needed a chaperon to stop me getting up to anything with a woman he didn't approve of.'

'Oh,' replied Jet, not knowing quite what to say. And then, to change the subject, 'How long ago did your mother die? He must miss her very much.'

Seth, who was sitting beside her on the soft brown leather sofa, stiffened perceptibly and seemed to draw himself away. For a long time he didn't answer, and when Jet looked up at him she saw that there were lines she hadn't seen before etched deeply at the corners of his mouth. 'No,' he said harshly. 'He's learned to stop missing her at last. He's had a lot of practice.'

Jet didn't understand, but she knew that she had inadvertently touched on a sensitive nerve. 'I'm sorry,' she murmured. 'I didn't mean to pry...'

'It's all right.' His voice was still iron hard, but Jet saw that his anger wasn't really directed at her. 'There's no reason you shouldn't know. My mother isn't dead. The fact is she left my father at least a dozen times before leaving him for good about five years ago. She's married to a lawyer in Seattle now, but he's only the last—I suppose—of a long line of alternatives to Father.'

'Alternatives to... oh, dear.' She *had* opened a Pandora's box when she brought up the subject of Seth's mother.

'Yes. Oh, dear.' Seth's tone was cruelly sarcastic now, and his fingers tapped angrily against the leather arm of the sofa. 'She led my father one hell of a dance all the time I was growing up. She'd be home for a while, and then I'd come back from school some evening and find she had vanished again. She told my father she needed a career, so he set her up first in a *knitting* shop, if you can imagine it—that lasted all of three months, then in an exclusive fashion boutique—that lasted a little longer, and then... Oh, I don't know.' He ran a hand distractedly through his hair. 'Then in a succession of equally unsuccessful ventures which she hadn't the tenacity, sense or self-control to make a go of. In the end she gave up the idea of a career as easily as she gave up everything else, and went off with that poor besotted bastard in Seattle.' His lips twisted. 'She's still a remarkably pretty woman.'

'Your poor father,' said Jet softly, putting a consoling hand on his arm. 'Poor you, too. It must have been very hard never knowing whether you had a mother at home or not.'

He shrugged. 'I got used to it. As you got used to the fact that your aunt and uncle didn't really want you. At least my father was always there when I needed him—like a rock in a sea of confusion.'

Jet nodded. 'Yes, that must have helped a lot.'

'It did most of the time.' There was still something bleak and distant about him, and Jet wondered what might be coming next. Then he gave her an odd, brief glance and grated out, 'He couldn't help me much when I fell for a girl exactly like Mother, though. He saw all the pitfalls and tried to warn me away, but of course I wouldn't listen. I was only nineteen and I was going to marry Lisa.'

'And did you?'

'No, but the only thing that stopped me was that she fell for someone else before I could pin her down. Luckily for me. Although it was a long time before I accepted that it *was* lucky.' He was staring straight ahead at a non-existent spot on the wall, and Jet's heart lurched with sympathy for the young man he had been.

'Yes,' she whispered. 'At nineteen, it's hard to see things like that clearly.'

And at twenty-five, she thought, looking at the unbearably attractive face beside her and knowing that she would never see things clearly either where Seth happened to be concerned.

What she did see, very clearly, was that it was no wonder that the young boy growing up in that wildly unstable household, who in the first flush of youth had fallen for a woman as flighty as his mother, should have turned into the severe, controlled, stern individual she had first encountered. Nor was it surprising that that same cold and clear-headed man should have made a careful and well-planned decision to marry the cool and sensible Marian, who knew precisely what she wanted and arranged to get it. The only thing which was at all surprising was that somehow things had not quite worked out as expected.

Jet's hand stole tentatively from his arm to his cheek, and she ran her fingers gently along the hard line of his jaw. He turned towards her, the bleakness

slowly leaving his eyes, as his hand came up to cover
hers.

'Well, butterfly,' he said softly, his lips parting
in a smile which melted every bone in her body,
'now that you've been introduced to all the family
skeletons, what do you think of the Hagans?'

'The same as I thought before,' replied Jet, not
taking her eyes off him.

'And what was that?'

'That one of them is a charmer and the other a
maddening, frustrating, distracting—and utterly
irresistible man.'

His smile grew broader, and Jet felt she was being
drawn right into the melting depth of his eyes. The
hand which covered hers turned her palm upwards
and covered it with soft kisses.

'You're beautiful, butterfly,' he murmured, as
his free arm moved determinedly around her waist.

When his kiss came, at first it was soft and gentle
like a summer breeze caressing the tops of trees,
but as her body responded to his closeness and she
sank further back into the sofa, pulling him down
on top of her, it became firmer, more passionate,
and when his hand moved under the black sweater
to cup her breast she heard a voice which could not
possibly be hers cry out, 'Seth, Seth, I—Seth,
please...'

And instantly, devastatingly, his hand was removed, her sweater was pulled roughly down and
he sat up.

'I apologise,' he rasped, in a voice which was not
quite steady.

Oh, lord, what was the matter now? 'There's
nothing to apologise for,' she responded truthfully,
struggling to recover her breath and pushing herself

into a sitting position as she edged as far away from him as she could. 'I—I like you kissing me, Seth.'

Seth pushed a hand through his unusually dishevelled hair and then ran it across his forehead. 'Yes. Yes, I know. I'm sorry.'

'What are you sorry for?' asked Jet in a small voice.

Seth stood up abruptly and began pacing around the room. Then he turned to stare at her, laughed shortly and said he was damned if he knew himself.

'I think,' said Jet quietly, 'that you do know. You started to kiss me, then remembered I wasn't Marian. That's really what's bothering you, isn't it?'

For a moment he just glared at her, and she was forced to restrain herself from running to throw her arms around her, because he looked so male and magnificent, all smouldering and glowering like that. Then he shrugged, smiled tightly and said that perhaps she was right.

A few minutes later they were driving back across the bridge in a funny, brittle sort of silence which left far too much unsaid. And Seth, with a slightly malicious look in her direction, was lighting a cigarette.

'Goodnight, Jet,' he said when he dropped her at her door. He touched her cheek briefly and strode quickly back to his car.

'Goodnight, Seth,' she whispered, as she grovelled in her bag for her keys. Infuriatingly, just because she wanted to get inside quickly, and because she knew he was sitting in the car watching her, this had to be the time that her fingers grasped everything she owned except the recalcitrant keys. Lipstick, pens, two plastic spoons, a plaster, something hard which was probably that stone she had picked up on the beach two days ago, and finally, thankfully, her keys which, inevitably, the way this evening was going, took a full two minutes to insert into the lock.

And then at last she was inside, and she heard Seth's engine start up as he drove quickly away down the street.

It was Friday morning. For the past two days Jet had felt as depressed and apathetic as she had been after the affair with Joe and Mr Allison. But once again, and as she had been doing all her life, she knew it was time to take a deep breath, lift her chin, put a smile on her face and go out to take on the world. She might be dying inside, but that was nothing new, nothing she couldn't handle.

She tried not to think about Seth, but as usual it didn't work. What *had* happened that evening at his house? Why had he been so tender and loving one moment, and then leaping up in a fury the next? She had asked him that, hadn't she? And he had said he didn't know. Jet sighed. Maybe he really didn't know, but it was all too obvious to her. He had missed Marian, tried to console himself with the woman he thought of as a butterfly, and then felt guilty about it. She nodded to herself. Yes, that would be just like Seth. His moral code and his conscience would be bound to get in the way of any sort of temporary dalliance. Maybe that hadn't been the case once, but now—now he was an older, harder and much more cynical man. And his cynicism would be directed at himself as much as anyone else.

It was strange that Seth hadn't mentioned the baby again, though. He had seemed so horrified when she first told him about it, but afterwards he had dismissed the matter as if it were almost of no account. Strange. Shaking her head and giving up on the mystery, Jet reached absently for a glass tray on top of her small chest of drawers.

Her fingers closed around a lipstick. Damn. Wrong colour. She tried her handbag. No luck there, either. She had just pushed aside a pile of cutlery in the kitchen drawer to discover the lipstick lurking coyly beneath a fish fork, when the telephone rang.

Jet sighed impatiently and picked it up.

'Hi,' said an achingly familiar voice. 'I wanted to phone you yesterday, but I had to go over to Victoria.' When she didn't answer, he added quickly, 'Are you still speaking to me, butterfly?'

CHAPTER EIGHT

'No,' said Jet automatically. 'I'm not.'

'I see. You could have fooled me.' There was an ill-concealed edge of laughter of Seth's voice, and in spite of herself Jet responded.

'I guess that did sound ridiculous, didn't it?' She chuckled, and relief washed over her in a dizzying wave because he hadn't written her off, after all. 'Of course I'm speaking to you, Seth. Why wouldn't I be?'

'Because I behaved like an idiot the other night. You were so warm and sweet, and I treated you like...'

'A piece of fish that's gone unexpectedly bad,' Jet finished for him.

'Well, I wouldn't have put it quite that way.'

'I would.'

'Yes. So you would.' He was making no attempt to control the laughter now, and Jet was just beginning to catch his mood when he added unbelievably, 'Listen, I'd like to make amends. I have to go back to Victoria on Monday. I'm thinking of setting up a branch office over there—and I was hoping you would come with me.'

Jet's laughter died in her throat. '*What* did you say?' she asked cautiously.

'I asked if you would come to Victoria with me. Just for a few days. You need a holiday, anyway.'

'Oh, do I? Who says?' asked Jet belligerently, her hackles rising immediately for no other reason

than that Seth was telling her what she needed
again. First food, then a husband—and now a
holiday.

'I do,' replied Seth calmly, causing Jet's blood
pressure to soar even further.

'Well, I *don't*.'

'Right. I'll pick you up at twelve o'clock
tomorrow, then. That way we can spend the
afternoon and Sunday looking around Victoria, I'll
finish my business on Monday and we'll come home
on the evening ferry.'

'Like hell we will.'

'Don't swear. It's unbecoming.'

'Don't preach. It's boring.'

Seth's prolonged sigh floated audibly down the
wires. 'You make a point of being unreasonable,
don't you, sweetheart? No, there's no need to
answer,' he added quickly, as she started to ex-
postulate. 'I'll pick you up at noon tomorrow.'

'Oh, no, you . . .'

But the phone had already gone dead.

Jet glared at it. So he'd pick her up at noon,
would he? Just like that? As if she had no say in
the matter whatever? Well, if he thought she was
going to be here when he came tomorrow . . . he was
absolutely right. She'd be here, if only to give him
a forthright piece of her mind.

Who do you think you're kidding, Jet Kellaway?
she muttered to herself as she rescued her missing
lipstick from beneath the fish fork. You'll be here
because you want to see that impossible hunk again.
And you know it.

Oh, yes, she knew it all right. But that didn't
make it any easier to take. She kicked disgustedly
at a bottle of Coke sitting beside the waste bin on

the floor, missed it and stubbed her toe against the wall.

'And it's all your fault, Seth Hagan,' she grumbled as she pulled off a shoe to investigate the damage. It's not, said another voice inside her, it's your own for falling for that aggravating man.

But, aggravating or not, the next day he was on her doorstep promptly at twelve o'clock. When she heard his peremptory knock she stared at the door for a moment, thought about pretending she was out—for at least two seconds—and then went to open it.

Seth's deep brown eyes swept over her appraisingly. 'Hm. Yes, you'll do,' he nodded, leaning comfortably against the wall with his ankles crossed, taking in her neatly fitting pink slacks and T-shirt at a glance.

Jet stared at him, for once at a loss for a sharp retort. 'So will *you*,' she breathed, her eyes running incredulously from his waving brown hair to the soft grey suede jacket over a white fleeced sweatshirt, to the tight jeans which encased his hips and thighs, and finally, down to the grey leather boots on his feet. 'You...you look so different—so—so...'

The word she wanted was sexy, but she was damned if she was going to admit it.

'Irresistible?' he suggested. His face was sober, but there was a mocking gleam in his eye that made Jet want to slap his self-satisfied face—if she could only keep her hands off the rest of him.

'No. Conceited,' she told him, as common sense took over again. 'And arrogant and dictatorial. You can't just order me to go on holiday with you, Seth.'

'Can't I?' His eyes ran over her again, and now the gleam was even more pronounced. 'But I see you're dressed for the ferry. And there's something lurking behind that chair that looks a lot like a travelling bag.' He crossed his arms over his chest and leaned his head back. 'Besides, if I hadn't been arrogant and dictatorial, you'd have gone on insisting you couldn't come.' He smiled disarmingly. 'Wouldn't you?'

And suddenly all Jet's resentment evaporated, and she laughed. 'Yes,' she agreed, 'I expect I would. But I still don't see... Seth...?'

'*Now* what is it?' he asked, as he saw her hang her head and scuff her shoe across the floor like a little girl caught at the cookie jar.

'Seth, we're not—I mean, I'm not...'

In one stride he was across the floor and had her in his arms. 'You're not what?' he asked, laughing down into her face.

She raised her eyes very slowly, disturbingly conscious of his arms around her waist and his body pinning her close. 'We're not going to—sleep...'

'Aren't we?' His eyes regarded her teasingly. 'How very exhausting.'

'Oh, Seth, you know I didn't mean that.'

Hearing the distress in her voice, Seth suddenly relented. 'I know what you meant,' he said smiling. 'I won't try to seduce you, butterfly. I promise.'

'You wouldn't get the opportunity,' said Jet, reddening slightly.

'I know,' he agreed soothingly. But, as his arms dropped down below her waist and his hands brushed lightly over her bottom, Jet wasn't at all sure that it was true he wouldn't get the opportunity.

* * *

As the Corvette followed the long line of ferry traffic down the Pat Bay highway to Victoria, Seth looked across at Jet and smiled.

'I told you you needed a holiday,' he said smugly. 'You've looked much happier and more relaxed since we left that depressing flat of yours behind us.'

Jet felt a momentary flash of annoyance. It was all very well for this comfortable, successful man to criticise her flat, but *he* had never known what it was like to live on very little money. Then she relaxed again. He was right. Her basement *was* depressing. It was a beautiful sunny day, she was going to spend two more beautiful days with the man she loved—and she was much too happy to quarrel.

'Yes,' she agreed, smiling back at him. 'I always loved sailing through Active Pass and the islands. Especially on a day like today. It makes me feel as though I'm a tourist at the start of a cruise round the world.'

Seth grinned. 'You have grandiose ideas, Miss Kellaway, for a woman who just wanted to teach children.'

'I'm a dreamer.'

He glanced at her again and his brown eyes filled with a tenderness Jet didn't see because she was staring at a flock of starlings beside the road. 'Yes, I believe you are,' he said quietly. And then, after a while, 'Tell me, have you made this trip often before? Somehow I had the impression...'

'That my life has not been one long holiday? You're right, it hasn't. But Aunt Sadie and Uncle Joe used to come over to Vancouver Island sometimes when I was young.' She made a face. 'They couldn't very well leave me behind. I haven't been here since I was a child, though.'

'You don't see your aunt and uncle any more, do you? Did they die?' He asked the question quite matter-of-factly, as though it were of no particular importance, but somehow it wasn't offensive.

'Oh, no,' replied Jet. 'They moved up to Squamish just before I lost the baby.'

'That's not very far away.'

'I know. I usually see them at Christmas. That's really quite often enough for all of us.' She gave a sad little smile which caused Seth to tighten his lips and plot suitably violent ends for Jet's relations.

He stretched a hand across the seat and patted her on the thigh. 'Poor kid,' he murmured. The impulse which had made him touch her in the first place had been almost paternal, but now, as their eyes met briefly, both of them were suddenly aware that any physical contact between them aroused feelings which had nothing remotely to do with any kind of family relationship.

'I'm not a kid,' Jet protested breathlessly.

'You can say that again.' Seth kept his eyes on the road. 'Jet?'

'Mm?'

'What happened, when you had the baby? You must have been very young.'

So he *had* been thinking about what she had told him, and for once Jet didn't feel like saying it was none of his business. Because somehow it *was* his business. But not here, not in a car which was finally gathering speed as Seth passed several trucks loaded with wood, and a sedan with a sign in the back saying 'Drive carefully. Baby on Board'. As if people would automatically crash into it if there wasn't a baby on board, thought Jet disparagingly.

But Seth was waiting for an answer.

'I wondered why you didn't ask before,' she said quietly, knowing she was prevaricating.

'I'm not sure,' he replied thoughtfully. 'Partly because it was more your affair than mine, partly because I knew the subject must hurt you, and...' he smiled sardonically, 'mostly, I suppose, because I didn't really get the chance. The timing always seemed to be wrong.'

'Truth will out,' murmured Jet drily. She stared at a small shopping centre beside the road, not seeing it, then added slowly, 'I will tell you, Seth. But later. Somewhere where I won't have to share your attention with the traffic.'

He nodded. 'OK. I know just the spot. Or are you hungry?'

Jet laughed. 'I don't know where you get the idea that I have my beak permanently open for food. We ate on the ferry.'

'Yes, but you can't call that eating.'

'You can if you've lived on peanut butter for weeks. After that, the ferry hamburgers and fries don't taste too bad at all.'

'I suppose not,' agreed Seth, mentally berating himself. He kept forgetting that in some ways Jet's life had been very different from his.

Half an hour later he steered the Corvette slowly along the edge of Beacon Hill Park, enjoying Jet's face as she gazed delightedly at the flowers. Then he pulled to a stop on a grassy headland far above the Strait of Juan de Fuca.

'Come on,' he said, hauling her out of the car to stand beside him. He put his arm round her waist and held her against him. When he felt her shiver, he turned his head and saw that the wind was blowing her long dark hair about her like a storm cloud. And she wasn't wearing a coat.

'Cold?' he asked softly. 'Here, take my jacket, I've got more on than you.'

Yes, thought Jet, more's the pity. And then she stopped herself, trying not to laugh aloud. If either of them had less clothes on in this howling gale, they would surely both freeze to death.

Seth led her down the steeply sloping headland to a little hollow with stunted bushes on three sides. He dropped easily to the ground and motioned her to join him. But when she ignored his gesture he took her hand imperiously and pulled her down beside him. His arm encircled her suede-clad shoulders, and suddenly she felt much too warm. The wind couldn't reach them down here.

'All right,' he said, settling her comfortably against the hillside as they gazed out over the frothing blue-grey waters far below. 'All right, butterfly. Now tell me.'

Jet stared intently at the sea as her mind went back nine years to the time when she had first met Gino.

'I was sixteen,' she began slowly. 'My aunt and uncle kept telling me to take all the practical courses at school, and I wouldn't because I wanted to go on to university. So they got angry, and said I needn't think *they* were paying. I knew they just wanted to get me into a job and off their hands as soon as they possibly could. So we argued a lot, and things were worse than usual around the house. My cousins sat listening to all the arguments and enjoying every moment, and that just made it worse.' She tugged at a blade of grass and it broke. 'Then Gino started to take an interest in me. He lived down the street and was seven years older than I was. He said he loved me, and he tried to—he wanted to...'

'Go to bed with you,' Seth interrupted roughly.

'Yes.' Jet watched a towering wave crash against the rocks and shatter into diamonds. 'Yes. Only I wouldn't. I loved him, though. I was crazy about him. Nobody had ever said they loved *me* before, you see. In the end, he said he wanted to marry me. Looking back, I think it was because that was the only way he could—could...'

Seth said something crude, in a voice Jet hadn't heard him use before. She flinched, and then agreed wryly that yes, that just about put Gino's motives in a nutshell.

'And did you agree to marry him? What about your aunt and uncle?'

'Oh, they were ecstatic. Marriage would get me off their hands faster than anything else they could think of. And yes, of course I agreed. I was in love. Or I thought I was.'

'And what about university?' Seth still sounded as though he wanted to hit somebody. Jet hoped it wasn't her.

'At that point nothing seemed to matter except Gino—and getting out of that house. If I thought about it at all, I suppose I vaguely intended to finish my education later.'

'So you were married?'

'Yes. Very quietly, just two days after I turned seventeen. Three months later I was pregnant. Gino worked in a warehouse and gradually he kept coming home later and later every night. About six months after our wedding he said I had a lot of growing up to do and that he was tired of baby-sitting. Just before I lost my baby, he left.'

Seth made another unprintable remark. 'That young man needed to grow up some himself,' he said roughly, his arm tightening about Jet's shoulders. 'He also needed a good kick where it hurts. I hope I'll some day have the privilege.'

Jet turned her face to the side to look up at him. His expression was austere and forbidding—and just plain old-fashioned, and because Jet knew she was not the target of his wrath she almost felt like laughing.

'Don't worry about it,' she said lightly. 'I expect Gino is too far away to kick by now. I heard he moved to Saskatchewan and I haven't seen him for years.'

'Good.' Seth's tone was abstracted. 'Funny. When you first told me about your baby, I assumed you hadn't been married.'

'I know. And you disapproved.'

He shrugged. 'Oh, I don't know. I think I was just shocked. You seemed so young.'

'I was old enough.' Jet turned away from him and pulled up a whole handful of grass. 'Would it have made any difference, if I hadn't been married?'

She felt him stiffen. 'What do you mean?' His eyes met hers and held them, in a penetrating gaze from which she couldn't escape.

'I mean would you—despise me—if I hadn't been married? Would it matter?'

Scth swore again, and Jet reminded him that he had told her that kind of language was unbecoming.

'Sorry,' he growled, not sounding sorry at all. 'And no, you ridiculous little idiot. Of course it wouldn't matter a damn.'

It was not until much later that he realised that up until just a few weeks ago it would have mattered a very great deal. Before he met Jet, he had been quite sure that any woman who got into trouble had only herself to blame. But somehow he didn't think that way any more.

The sun was much lower in the sky by the time they left the grassy headland some hours later. As streaks of pewter alternated with burnt orange across the green-black surface of the sea, Seth remarked reluctantly that it was time they booked into their hotel and did something constructive about getting themselves a meal.

Jet nodded and stood up quickly, and as they walked hand in hand up the hill together—not nearly as quickly as they had come down—she thought that these past few hours had been the happiest of her life.

She and Seth had talked quietly, and with none of the strain of their previous encounters, about their childhoods, neither of which had been particularly happy, about Seth's business and her ambitions and what they enjoyed doing in their leisure time. They discovered that they both liked to read on a wide variety of subjects, and Jet learned that they shared a common love of the theatre. She also learned that Seth was a champion squash player and belonged to a local rugby club. At first this information had surprised her, because, although she had thought of him as high-powered and successful, she had not thought he was especially sports-minded. Then she remembered her first view of his hand holding open the door of his office, and how she had thought then that it was the sort of hand that would accomplish what it set out to do—and his sporting activities fell neatly into place as an integral part of the complex character of this man.

When they reached the car, Seth's fingers slipped briefly beneath her hair to caress the nape of her neck as he helped her in. And, as Jet felt the familiar sensations that his touch invariably aroused, she wondered how they had managed to sit quietly talking for so long without falling into an embrace. All that side of things seemed to be on hold, waiting for the right moment—the moment that she knew was drawing close.

Seth had booked adjoining rooms at the Empress Hotel overlooking Victoria's harbour. The hotel had been designed by Francis Rattenbury at the beginning of the century, and the mellow, ivy-covered building was now one of Victoria's best known landmarks. Mr Rattenbury had not fared as well, Jet remembered with a shudder, as she removed her few clothes from her bag. He had been murdered by his wife's young lover over in England and, when the lover had been sentenced, the unhappy wife had stabbed herself on the banks of the River Avon. For a moment something dark and heavy hung brooding over Jet's shoulder, and she felt a wave of empathy for that drowned, besotted woman. Then she shook the feeling off, glanced at the door which connected her room with Seth's, and went to check that it was locked.

It was. She smiled with a mixture of relief and disappointment. So Seth intended to keep his promise. She had been almost sure he would.

When, just as she was dressing, his knock came on the outside door, she hastily pulled on the only dress she owned which was less than four years old—a bright blue linen with open-work flowers on the bodice and a softly pleated skirt—and hurried to let him in.

'You look very lovely,' he smiled, his eyes roaming over her in leisurely appraisal. Then they widened, and she saw him put his hand up to his mouth. 'Mind you, I'm not sure it's safe to let you out like that. You're liable to be attacked by the first sex-starved male who sets eyes on you.' He grinned. 'And as I'm not feeling especially pugilistic this evening, do you think you could possibly make yourself at least passably decent before we attempt to go out? Not that I'm complaining, of course. The view is quite inspiring. In fact, I'm giving serious consideration to attacking you myself.'

'Wh-what?' gasped Jet, puzzled and completely nonplussed. 'But I *am* decent.' She glanced down at her skirt to see if it was caught up in her belt, or inexplicably ripped in an awkward place. But it was a model of bright blue decorum.

'I am decent,' she repeated. Then, as a sort of comprehension began to dawn, she asked doubtfully, '*Are* you sex-starved?'

'Moderately,' replied Seth drily. He put his hands on her shoulders and turned her to face the mirror, and she could feel the length of his body pressed against her back and his breath stirring her hair.

Then her hands flew up to hide the colour which she knew was streaming across her face. And to hide Seth's mocking eyes, which gazed out at her form the mirror. For, in her haste to let him in, she had forgotten to put on the slip which went under her dress, and beneath the pretty cut-out flowers of her bodice her breasts were visible for all the world to see. And at the moment all the world was Seth.

The mockery in his eyes deepened as his hands slipped down her shoulders to cover the cause of her embarrassment. And immediately a shock of desire went through her, making her gasp and lean back, rigid, against his powerful chest.

Seth, seeing her face in the mirror, closed his eyes, drew in his breath and pushed her gently away.

'It's all right, butterfly,' he soothed. 'No damage done. I'll look the other way while you put everything right.'

Jet, stifling a ridiculous urge to cry, sniffed and said there wasn't much point in his looking away, was there, since he'd already seen everything there was to see?

'Oh, yes, there is,' Seth contradicted feelingly. 'Believe me, if you want me to keep that promise, there's a very considerable point.'

Jet decided the conversation was getting uncomfortably close to the mark again, and, grabbing her slip and bra from a drawer, retreated with as much dignity as she could muster to the bathroom.

The restaurant Seth took her to was not far from the hotel, and in keeping with his seeming conviction that the undernourished Jet needed man-sized meals to stay alive, it specialised in enormous plates of deliciously barbecued spare ribs. As the waiter tied a large bib around her neck, Seth smiled and said she looked just like a little girl. But when the waiter came to tie one around *his* neck he waved him away, saying he didn't need it.

'But you think *I* do?' asked Jet in mock indignation.

'I'm sure of it,' he replied complacently.

And, irritatingly, he turned out to be absolutely right. As she nibbled each succulent morsel to the bone, small brown spots began to appear on her flowered bib. Seth, on the other hand, managed with maddening efficiency to consume just as much as she did without even appearing to eat.

When the waiter suggested dessert, Jet said virtuously that she'd had enough. But Seth had seen her eyes light up when she heard the words 'strawberry shortcake', and calmly ordered two portions.

'But I don't need it,' protested Jet reluctantly.

'Yes, you do. Eat up, there's a good girl.'

'Are you *sure* you've never been a father?' asked Jet sarcastically.

'Quite sure. But I'd like to be.'

Jet stared down at her plate. Seth's eyes narrowed, and somehow, after that, the comfortable, teasing companionship that they had shared all day seemed to disintegrate, and both of them became silent.

They finished their meal rather quickly, and Seth suggested they should go for a walk along the waterfront. When they rounded a corner, Jet's starry eyes fell on the lights outlining the great domed Parliament Buildings like some glittering fairy fantasy reflected in silver water. She gasped.

Seth glanced down at her. 'Haven't you seen them before?' he asked quizzically.

'No. Well, yes. But not at night time. It's beautiful.'

'There's so much you haven't seen, isn't there, butterfly?' His voice was deep and gentle, and Jet heard the tenderness behind his words, and for the second time that day she wanted to cry.

'I suppose there is,' she murmured. 'I just never had the chance. Maybe some day.'

'Maybe.' The warm baritone seemed suddenly harder, more enigmatic, and Jet drew away from the shelter of his arm.

A short time later they returned to the hotel, because Seth said they should get an early night so they would be refreshed and ready to explore Victoria in the morning.

Outside the door of Jet's room they paused, and their eyes met and spoke without any word passing between them. But what each wanted to acknowledge remained unsaid, and in what seemed like only an instant of time Seth had taken Jet's arms, bent his head to kiss her very lightly on the forehead, murmured 'Goodnight, butterfly,' and disappeared.

Jet, her heart thumping so loudly she was sure he must have heard it, closed her door behind her and slumped down on the bed.

She spent an uncomfortably restless night tossing from side to side and glaring resentfully at the summer moon which glimmered in a chink between the curtains. Finally, some time between three and four in the morning, she drifted off to sleep, only to dream that a warm, hard body lay beside her, its arms draped casually across her breast.

'Gino?' she murmured out loud, feeling more surprise than pleasure. Then she realised the body had a face, and it wasn't Gino beside her, it was Seth. And she gave a sigh of contentment, nestled her head happily into his shoulder—and woke up.

The shoulder turned out to be the bunched-up spare pillow in the queen-sized bed. Jet pushed it away crossly, scowled at the unresponsive moon and sat up. The bed seemed suddenly enormous, and very empty. In the end she switched on the light and tried to read, so that dawn found her propped up on the pillows, her book lying opened and unread on the bed beside her, and her eyes, at last, peacefully closed.

She was awakened by a discreet tap on the door and the arrival of a breakfast tray. Seth, in his relentless determination to ensure that she ate enough, had apparently ordered for her. Scrambled eggs, bacon, hash brown potatoes, orange juice and coffee. Jet stared at this bounty in dismay. After years of starting the day with no more than a cup of coffee and possibly a slice of toast, she wasn't at all sure she could do justice to this impressive repast. But she thought she had better try. Otherwise she had a feeling she would have to listen to Seth lecturing her again. To her surprise, and somewhat to her discomfiture, in no time at all the eggs, bacon and potatoes seemed to have disappeared. She was just starting the coffee when there was another knock on the door. Hastily pulling on a thin blue cotton robe, Jet ran her fingers through her tousled hair and went to see who was there.

Seth stood on the threshold, smiling, looking revoltingly clean and awake and holding a cup of coffee.

'Can I join you?' he asked cheerfully. He sounded so bright and energetic that Jet felt like telling him she never spoke to anyone before noon. But instead she said rather sourly that she supposed since he was here he'd better come in.

'Your enthusiasm overwhelms me,' he remarked drily, as he settled into a chair and propped his feet on the bottom of the bed.

'You'll get the covers dirty,' was Jet's uncompromising response.

'No, I won't. My shoes aren't even touching them.'

'I might have known. *You* never get anything dirty, do you?'

Seth put down his cup, and suddenly retribution seemed disconcertingly close. 'You know what you're cruising for, butterfly.'

'I'm cruising for a bit of peace and privacy.'

'That wasn't what I had in mind. Are you always this charming in the morning?'

In spite of herself, Jet giggled. He looked so alive and male and filled with vitality, stretched out casually in her chair with his arms now resting behind his head. His jeans and soft beige sweatshirt were clean and uncreased, and compared to her he looked like an advertisement for morning.

'Sorry,' she murmured. 'I know I must look like a witch, but that's no excuse for behaving like one, too.'

'That's better,' said Seth approvingly. 'And if witches all look like you, they must be a very sexy lot.'

'Seth Hagan,' said Jet reprovingly, 'that's hardly the sort of remark I expect from the owner of a respectable employment agency.'

'Why not? I don't employ witches. Perhaps I should.'

Jet gave an exasperated sigh and said she was going to get dressed. And she wasn't quite sure but, as she grabbed an armful of clothes and stalked into the bathroom, she thought she heard him murmur, 'That's too bad.'

She shook her head. Seth had changed, he must have done. Or perhaps it was only as one got to know him that the warm, attractive man under the cold exterior finally began to emerge.

When she went back into the bedroom there was a cloud of smoke around Seth's head, and he was flipping through the book she had neglected on the bedspread.

'You're smoking,' she said accusingly.

'So I am. And you're a teller of tall tales.' He gestured at the book. 'This is *not* one of those literary classics or sober educational journals you told me you're so fond of reading.'

Jet grinned sheepishly. 'No, but it's nice light reading for a holiday.'

Seth lifted an eyebrow. 'You call this light?'

Jet looked over his shoulder and her eye fell on a particularly steamy and erotically charged paragraph. 'Oh,' she said hastily. 'Well it's not all like that, of course.'

'Like what?' He was being deliberately obtuse, she was sure of it, and if he wanted to be difficult she would give him exactly what he was asking for.

'Oh, you know. Hairy chest meets creamy-mounded breast. That sort of thing,' she explained blithely. She was staring at the top of his head and she could have sworn she saw his shoulders start to shake. But when he turned to look up at her his face was convincingly blank, and he only remarked with suspicious innocence that no, he didn't know about that sort of thing, but perhaps it was time he learned.

Jet took in the lean length of his body, still stretched out comfortably in the chair as though he was quite prepared to spend the day there. Then her eyes travelled to his face, and she saw a gleam in his heavy-lidded eyes which was anything but innocent.

'If we're going to see Victoria, I think we'd better get started, don't you, Seth?' she said a little too brightly.

'What's the rush?'

'No rush, it's just . . .' The gleam was more pronounced than ever, and Jet finished desperately, 'It's just that it's another nice day, and we don't want to waste it, do we?'

'Don't we?'

'Seth. Do come on.' She seized his hand and tried to dislodge him from the chair, and then felt foolish when he just sat there looking at her with a maddening little smile on his lips. She dropped his hand quickly and turned away. 'Of course, it you don't want to go out . . .' she muttered into the collar of her blue and green checked shirt.

Immediately Seth was on his feet and standing close behind her. 'I was only teasing, butterfly.' There was laughter in his voice as his arms came around her waist to press her gently against his chest. His chin rested for a moment on her hair and then he spun her around, kissed her quickly on the tip of her nose, spun her back again and pushed her ahead of him towards the door.

'My bag,' wailed Jet quickly. 'I can't go without my bag.'

'Why not? Are you packing the crown jewels in it, then?'

'No. Just my face.'

'Now wait a minute...'

'I mean my lipstick and powder and my comb and—and all those other essentials.' She gave him a slightly self-conscious smile.

'Gilding the lily,' Seth murmured flatteringly, as Jet rescued her bag from a drawer beside her bed. But when she looked at his face it seemed more impatient than admiring, and she decided she must have misheard.

The day was idyllic, and Jet cherished every moment of it as if it might be her last with Seth. As indeed after this weekend it might be, but she tried not to think of that. They drove out to Butchart's Gardens, Victoria's floral showplace and just now at the height of its colourful summer beauty. They wandered through the impressive Royal British Columbia Museum and the Crystal Gardens aviary which had once been Victoria's favourite swimming pool. They even had tea and crumpets at the Empress and felt like every other tourist pretending to be English in a city that never quite succeeded in being as English as it hoped it was. And after that, of course, they went to Beacon Hill Park to walk off the effects of the crumpets, so that they would be able to enjoy their dinner— this time delicate seafood in a restaurant overlooking the water. And they laughed a lot and teased each other gently—and were happy.

And at last, as the sun disappeared and the reflected lights shimmered across the harbour, they went back to the hotel, had a long cool drink in the bar, and finally, feeling tired and, in Jet's case at least, quite inexplicably shy, they made their way up to their rooms.

Once again they paused outside Jet's door. She was holding her key in her hand, but this time when their eyes met Seth didn't kiss her quickly and disappear. Instead his arms wrapped around her firmly, holding her against him as his cheek rested on her hair. For a moment they swayed together, eyes closed, lost in a world of their own which shut out the two mildly scandalised old ladies who passed them on the way to the lift. Then Seth's mouth moved down over hers and the emotions they had refused to recognise all day broke loose in a wild, explosive need for each other that made Jet cry out loud. It was a low, wordless cry like that of a small, soft animal. And, hearing it, Seth slowly let her go.

His hands were still on her waist, lightly now, and the eyes that looked down at Jet were wide and dark with desire. His hair was in waving disarray where her fingers had caught in it, and his skin was dark like his eyes, suffused by the heat of his blood.

'Jet, I can't—oh, hell.' His eyes closed briefly and he ran a hand round the back of his neck.

'Seth?' Her voice was the merest whisper.

For answer he suddenly reached for the keys which she was still clutching tightly. When his fingers touched her hand she released them, but when he turned the lock, pushed her in and started to close the door on her agonised face she gave a cry that this time was not low at all, pulled the handle from his grasp and gasped, 'No. No, Seth. Please—please don't go.'

A military gentleman passing in the passage gave them an indignantly disapproving glare, but neither of them even saw him.

Seth, still framed in the doorway, jerked his head at the ceiling, not looking at her. Then he stared down at the floor. 'Jet...' She saw his fists clench hard against his thighs as he said in a tight, controlled voice, 'Jet, I made a promise. If I don't go, I'm going to break it. And *that's* a promise.'

Jet moved her tongue slowly across her dry lips. Then she took a step towards him, put her hand on his wrist and drew him into her arms.

His hands were already exploring her body with a quiet but purposeful desperation as he kicked the door shut behind them, and she answered softly, 'I want you to break it, Seth. Please.'

CHAPTER NINE

SETH gave a low groan. 'Do you know what you're saying, butterfly?' he whispered.

'Yes,' she whispered back. 'Oh, yes, Seth. I know.'

He laughed, a wild, reckless sort of laugh, and suddenly she found herself caught up in his arms, carried across the room and deposited without ceremony on her back on top of the bed.

She stared up at him, her dark eyes wide and trusting, as, with a smile in which tenderness mingled seductively with passion, he threw off his jacket, lowered himself down beside her and took her very gently in his arms.

Jet sighed, a sigh of pure happiness, and placed her own arms around his neck where they belonged. And she gave to him as much as he gave to her, because her gift was everything she had.

As all the old images of stars and flames and waves exploded together and became for both of them the truth they had always been, Jet experienced a joy and beauty and happiness she had never known in the past. Somewhere at the back of her mind she remembered that years ago she had been along this road before. But not like this. Never like this, because then it had not been with Seth. And Seth was all she had ever hungered for without even knowing her need. But now she did know. And there would never be anyone but Seth. Not ever again.

When they lay together, sated and at peace, Seth propped himself on one elbow, smoothed back her long dark hair and smiled. And his smile was so deep and tender that she felt tears of joy pricking at the back of her eyes.

Jet trailed her fingers lovingly through the fine, soft hairs of his chest. 'I love you, Seth,' she said softly, because she wanted him to know.

A shadow passed momentarily across his face, and when he answered her, instead of saying, I love you, too, he said, 'You're very beautiful, sweetheart. The most beautiful butterfly I've known.'

Once again Jet felt something dark and unhappy lurking behind her shoulder, but she pushed it away and put her hand tenderly behind his head, pulling it down to lie beside hers on the pillow.

Soon, very soon, they made love again, and because they were still learning about each other, this time it was different, but just as miraculous and explosive as before.

Dawn was already sending pink messages across the sky when they finally fell asleep, exhausted and happy and locked in each other's arms.

Much later, when Jet struggled awake at last, the sun was beaming through the windows.

And Seth had gone.

She gave a little cry of distress and her eyes roamed frantically around the room as she swung her long legs over the side of the bed. Then, as swiftly as it had arisen, the tension in her body drained away.

The jacket which Seth had discarded so carelessly the night before still lay on the floor in a crumpled, untidy heap. So he couldn't have gone far.

Just then the door of her bathroom opened, and Seth, his skin damp, and still buttoning the sleeves of his shirt, came quickly into the room.

'You're awake.' He smiled at her, and if she noticed there was something withdrawn about the smile she was careful not to acknowledge it.

'Yes. For a moment I thought you'd gone.'

'Without even saying goodbye?' His lips still curved in a smile, but there was an edge to his voice that told Jet he resented the implication.

'No, I suppose...'

Then it hit her. Had he meant that he was really going to say goodbye? For a few hours? Or for always? She swallowed, trying to control her suddenly uneven breathing. And she knew that if she was going to have any peace of mind over the next few hours something very important had to be resolved between them.

'Seth...' she began slowly, almost afraid to speak.

'Mm hmm?' He was abstracted, standing in front of the mirror as he hurriedly knotted his tie.

'Seth—where do we go from here?'

'What?' He half turned towards her, his hands still at his neck and a slight furrow between his brows. 'What do you mean, from here? I explained it all last night. I'll pick you up somewhere around three o'clock. You said you'd spend a leisurely day walking in the park and having a look at the shops.' His eyes fell on his rumpled jacket, and with an impatient movement he bent to pick it up.

'No,' said Jet desperately. 'No, Seth, that's not what I'm talking about.'

He was easing the jacket over his shoulders now, and even in her distress Jet couldn't help noticing how fluidly he moved, and that the jacket was of

such good quality that there was almost no sign
that it had spent the night on the floor. But, as
much as she suddenly wanted to reach out to pull
him down beside her, she knew she must have an
answer from him first.

'What *are* you talking about, then?' he
demanded.

Why did she have this feeling he was almost
angry—or trying to evade her question?

'I'm talking about us, Seth. About the future.
You see, I need to know if we have one.'

Now she was sure he was angry, because instead
of replying he turned his back on her, walked over
to the window and pressed his hands flat against
the sill. 'Don't ask me that yet, Jet. I can't give
you the answer I think you want to hear.' He didn't
sound angry, after all, just tired and oddly
constrained.

Jet stared at his back, which was stooped slightly
but taut as strung out wire. She tried to speak, but
no words came, and in the end he was the one who
broke the silence as he turned abruptly to stare
down at her haggard, anxious face. 'Jet, I'm sorry.
Last night was—incredible.' He smiled bleakly. 'But
I've got a meeting in about twenty minutes, and
I'm afraid I'm late already. Can we please talk
about this later?'

It sounded reasonable. But why did she have this
conviction he was trying to hide something, trying
not to tell her the truth? The truth she was afraid
she already knew too well. She wanted to cry out,
to scream and kick at him and throw the tantrum
he had once accused her of having. But she didn't.
With a stupendous effort of will, she forced a
strained smile on to her lips and nodded calmly.

'Yes, of course. I'll see you later on, then, when you come back to pick me up.'

If he was trying to let her down gently, she was not going to let him know to just what depths of loss and loneliness she had fallen.

Jet heard him release his breath on a long sigh of relief.

'Good girl.' He took a step towards her, then seemed to change his mind. 'Till three o'clock, then.' He lifted his hand in a gesture of farewell, and in another moment the door had snapped firmly closed behind him.

Jet stared straight ahead at the spot where he had been standing. The swish of the door had stirred the air in the room, and as it whispered over her shoulders she was suddenly conscious of cold. She gazed, stupefied, at the goose-bumps on her bare thighs, and it was only then that it dawned on her that she had been carrying on a desperately important conversation perched on the edge of the bed she had shared with Seth—and that she did not have even a stitch of clothing on.

And he had not even tried to touch her.

Jet breakfasted on a piece of toast which almost choked her, and a great many cups of coffee. Then she dressed slowly and set off glumly for the town. Seth had not actually said they had no future together. But he *had* said he couldn't give her the answer she wanted to hear. That could only mean one thing: that, although she had told him she loved him, he was unable to return that love. Of course, she had always known his was only a temporary parting from Marian. And, even if it wasn't, why would a man like Seth want to spend the rest of his life with a woman he thought of as a flighty butterfly? A butterfly who couldn't have children. Oh, he liked her all right. She amused him. And last night had proved he wanted her as well. But that wasn't love, that was a different matter altogether.

Jet glared malevolently at a necklace of British Columbia jade in a shop window. Then she saw that the owner was staring at her with bright, suspicious eyes, and when the woman's hand reached for the phone she hurried quickly up the street.

She thought of the long hours stretching between now and three o'clock, when Seth would fetch her and drive her home. She supposed he had wanted her to come to Victoria in the first place so he would have someone to help him forget about Marian for a while. She had suspected that when he'd first suggested the trip, hadn't she? And soon he would dump her back at her door like a piece of baggage which had outlived its usefulness. So why had she agreed to come? She darted quickly around an odd little woman in a hat who was warding off the sun with an umbrella. Yes. Well, she knew the answer to that one too, didn't she? She had come because she loved Seth—who, having caught an unhappy butterfly in his net, was now about to release her. But it was too late, because she no longer wanted to be free.

And suddenly she knew she couldn't bear it. She couldn't wait all day for Seth to reappear, then go home with him on the ferry, knowing all the while that this was the end of the affair. Last night had been wonderful. She could never regret that. And she would always remember Seth as he had looked at her then, with such tenderness and passion. But she couldn't face him this afternoon in the cold light of reality, with that glint of discomfort and avoidance in his eye.

She stopped in her tracks and swung around, promptly colliding with a tall young man carrying an armload of parcels.

'For heaven's sake, watch what you're——' The young man stopped abruptly as he took in her wide, sad eyes, swinging dark brown hair and, thanks to Seth's determination to feed her, alluringly curving figure.

Jet saw his look of stunned appreciation, and as she murmured an apology and hurried away she found that the admiration helped. She might have lost Seth, but she was still an attractive woman. A woman who could accomplish something. Maybe she could never have children or be married as other women were, but she *could* help others to be happy. And for once in her life she could finish what she started to do.

Straightening her shoulders and lifting her chin bravely, she returned to the hotel to pack her clothes. An hour and a half later she was seated on a bus as it sped her towards the ferry to Vancouver.

And if, by some incredible chance, she was wrong, if Seth really did care for her after all, then he would surely phone her tonight when he read the brief note she had left him by her bed. Although—she tightened her lips—she was *not* going to be fool enough to hold her breath waiting for that unlikely call to come.

But of course she did hold it. She held it all that evening as she sat alone and desolate in her basement listening to John and Daisy being comfortably domestic next door. And she held it most of the following day, too. After all, Seth might have returned on the last ferry and decided it was too late to call.

By ten o'clock on Tuesday evening, she had all but given up. Obviously Seth had read her note, perhaps been grateful that she was making it easy for him, and come to the relieved conclusion that he hadn't hurt her too much, after all, and now was the time to let her go.

Wearily Jet pulled off her clothes and went through the nightly chore of making up her bed. She was sure she wouldn't sleep. But contrary to Seth's assertion that Victoria would be restful, it had proved exactly the opposite and she was really unbelievably tired. In no time at all her eyelids were drooping and she had fallen into a deep and dreamless sleep.

The next day passed in a mist of despair and loneliness. Even when she had lost the baby, Jet couldn't remember having experienced quite this depth of desolation. But that had been a different kind of loss. And now, in spite of her unhappiness, behind the very real grief was a thin, tough thread of determination that this time she would not allow events to defeat her. If Seth had done nothing else, he had at least inspired in her some reserve of strength that she had never known she possessed. Perhaps it was because he had once said he had faith in her that she now had faith in herself.

Jet glanced at her watch. It was probably wrong as usual, but still, by this time Daisy should be home. And she needed someone to talk to.

When she banged on the wall and shouted that she was coming over, Daisy shouted back that she could if she liked, but John was fast asleep with nothing on—or he had been until Jet woke him up. Guiltily Jet subsided on to a kitchen chair and a few minutes later Daisy was knocking on her door.

'Tell John I'm sorry,' Jet murmured as she ushered her friend in.

Daisy grinned. 'Sure. He'll get over it. Serves him right, anyway. He was up until four a.m. last night—watching an old war movie.'

Jet gave her a watery smile. 'At least you know what you'll have to look forward to if you two ever decide to get married.'

'Huh,' snorted Daisy. 'That'll be the frosty Friday morning.'

'Will it? Don't you approve of marriage?'

Daisy shrugged. 'I don't know. Maybe one day, when I've finished my degree and have my very own successful law practice.' Then, taking in Jet's dark, strained eyes and drooping dejected posture, she added sharply, 'Why? Don't tell me you're taking a sudden deplorable interest in orange blossom and white dresses? It's not improving your appearance any if you are.'

'Thanks. No, no orange blossom for me. Anyway, I much prefer daisies.'

'Mm. For obvious reasons I'm fond of them myself.' She sat down solidly at the small kitchen table and waved at the opposite chair. 'Now, you sit down over there, Jetta, and tell me what's eating you. Is it that man? The one John was grumbling to me about?'

Jet nodded. 'Yes. Seth. I spent the weekend with him in Victoria.'

'Sounds all right so far. Was he nice?'

'Very.'

'But he's not nice any more? John didn't take to him at all.'

'I'm not surprised. John saw him at his worst, and his worst can be very unpleasant.'

'Can it? Is that the problem?' Daisy reached her hand across the table and patted Jet's tightly clenched fist.

Jet glanced down at it in surprise and slowly unclenched her fingers. 'No. The problem is, I've fallen in love with him. And he doesn't love me back.'

'Fool,' scoffed Daisy. 'He must be crazy. Are you sure?'

'Oh, yes.' Jet related the events of the past few months, how she had first met Seth, how he kept appearing and disappearing in her life and how, finally, he had taken her to Victoria, made love to her—and then wondered how he could gracefully let her go.

'Hmm. Doesn't sound promising,' admitted Daisy. 'Still, you ought to give him a chance, Jetta. He could be angry because you ran away. Why don't you phone him?'

Jet shook her head. 'It's too late. He lives with his father, and the old man's probably asleep.'

'Yes. Just like the young man next door,' snorted Daisy, tossing her head disgustedly at the wall. 'So phone him tomorrow, then.'

Jet nodded. 'Perhaps you're right.' She desperately wanted Daisy to be right. 'OK. I'll phone him. Tomorrow.'

But when tomorrow came, and she awoke in the morning to see a thin beam of sunlight filtering through the window, she decided that she couldn't just phone Seth and talk to his disembodied voice.

In spite of her resolution to remember him as he had been in Victoria, she had to see his face just one more time.

Her mind made up, and with something concrete to do, she charged about the room like an indecisive whirlwind, putting on first her pink slacks, then the yellow dress and, finally, her beloved red flowered skirt—which as long as she kept it would bring memories of that night she was beginning to think had been nothing but a dream.

She knew Seth always arrived at work promptly at eight-thirty, and by ten past eight she was waiting across the street. At eight twenty-five the gold Corvette slid into the car park.

Her heart pounding and her mouth suddenly dry, Jet watched Seth park, swing easily out of his seat—and walk round to the right side of the car. And the pounding of her heart became deafening as she saw him open the door smoothly and reach in to help someone out.

The someone was a tall, leggy and exceptionally lovely blonde, younger than Marian and with a sweet, sexy smile—which she was now turning on Seth at full power. Jet's hands grabbed frantically at a lamp-post for support as Seth returned the smile and bent his head to whisper something in her ear. In a moment he had taken the blonde's arm and was leading her possessively up the steps to his office door.

Jet watched the broad back disappear for the last time, took a long breath, and with considerable effort detached herself from the lamp-post and made her way back to the bus.

Upstairs in his office, Seth happened to glance out of the window. When he caught a glimpse of a familiar red flowered skirt vanishing into the crowd that milled about on the pavement, he muttered an abrupt apology to the woman standing expectantly by his side and, taking the stairs three steps at a time, hurled himself outside into the street.

But, when he reached the place where he had seen her, Jet was no longer anywhere in sight.

'Hell!' he exclaimed loudly. This was followed by a string of profanity that made several passersby glance at him disapprovingly, and others stare in alarm as they looked round hopefully for the long arm of the law. When Seth saw a red-faced old gentleman bearing down on him brandishing an umbrella, he recollected his surroundings, muttered something which was mercifully inaudible, and strode furiously back across the street.

CHAPTER TEN

Wearily Jet dragged the last of her battered suit-
cases up the narrow stairway to her new apartment.
It was brighter than the one she had rented in
Vancouver, and from the window overlooking the
Dallas Road she could see the grey water of the
Strait. It was overcast today, dull and brooding and
in keeping with her mood. But she was sure she had
made the right decision.

After seeing Seth with his new blonde, she had
gone straight home to explain to a surprisingly
understanding landlord that she had to move
straight away, but would pay him till the end of
next month. Then, with a speed of which she had
not known she was capable, she had packed up all
her belongings except the furniture which came with
the flat. A few hours later she drove aboard the
ferry to Victoria.

Earlier, as she'd attempted to stuff two bulging
bags into her rented car, Daisy and John had
erupted frantically on to the scene.

'Hey. Where do you think you're going, without
even saying goodbye?' Daisy's indignant voice
broke in on Jet's grim concentration as she tried to
fit the bags inside the boot.

'I'm sorry.' Jet straightened. 'I would have
written. But—Daisy, I really have to get away. I
can't bear this place any more. Too many...' She
paused, and gripped the handle of the car. 'Too
many memories.'

'No orange blossom—or daisies?' her friend enquired sympathetically.

'No. No daisies. Just holly and hawthorne and nettles.'

'He's not worth it, Jetta,' John interposed with conviction. 'Stay here with your friends and forget him.'

Jet tried to smile, grateful for his support, but she only managed a grimace. 'I'll never forget him. And he is worth it,' she insisted. 'I'd like to stay here, John, but I think my only hope of sanity right now is to get away. Somewhere I've been happy, but somewhere I won't keep hoping he may call. And I've decided to go to university. I think a small one like Victoria will be best.'

John and Daisy continued to remonstrate with her, but nothing they said could move Jet from her resolve. In the end, and with great reluctance, they waved her regretfully on her way.

The last thing Jet made them promise as she started up the engine was that if Seth, stricken with an unexpected attack of conscience, should ask them where she had gone, they would not under any circumstances let him know. That, she decided sadly, was the only thing she could do now for the man she loved.

Jet spent the remainder of the summer settling in to her new apartment, exploring Victoria—mostly on foot—and ransacking the libraries for books that would refresh her memory of the subjects she had studied nine years before. To her great relief, although she had been late applying for entrance to the University of Victoria, her marks at school had been sufficiently impressive to secure her a place in first year. Money, she knew, was going to be a problem, but she still had some left from her time with Gourmet Distributors, and she had managed to obtain a student loan. If necessary, she could find a job dishwashing at the weekends.

When September came, at first she found it hard to get into the routine of studying again after so many years of reading purely for pleasure. But she had a goal now and she worked towards it with grim, unswerving tenacity. Her books were the only things which kept her mind off Seth, and the happiness she had lost almost as soon as she'd found it.

For a while everything went well. Jet noticed that she often felt tired now, and that she seemed to have lost some of the zest for living which had carried her through all the bad times in the past. But she put the feeling of lethargy and heaviness down to the emptiness that she supposed would always be with her now that Seth was no longer a part of her life.

She made a few new friends in her apartment building and at college, and they all tried to boost her spirits and persuade her that she needed some form of relaxation. It was one of these friends, a girl several years younger than herself called Lara, who finally remarked to her towards the middle of October that she really ought to visit a doctor.

'A doctor? Whatever for?' Jet was genuinely puzzled.

'Because when I first met you, although you seemed a little sad and pensive sometimes, you were reasonably bright and healthy. These last couple of weeks you've been looking like something the cat dragged in and rejected.'

'That bad?' Jet smiled disbelievingly.

'Worse.'

But still Jet paid no attention to her friend's insistence that something was wrong—until she found herself being sick three mornings in a row. That was odd. A long time ago she had been this route before, but then there had been a reason. This time that reason wasn't possible.

She continued to labour on with her studies for another week, still fighting sickness every morning, before it occurred to her that her bouts of nausea were not the only things that were odd. She started counting days on the calendar and her eyes widened in concern. Lara was right. Something was radically amiss.

The doctor was a slight, middle-aged man with a beard, and a bit of a fixation about nutrition. But he was kind and thorough, and after a careful examination he told Jet cheerfully that he was almost certain she was pregnant.

'But I can't be!' she wailed. 'It's not possible.'

'Oh, dear. It's like that, is it?' The doctor shook his head regretfully. 'My dear, I'm afraid that's what they all say. There really is very little doubt.'

'No, you don't understand.' Jet twisted the handle of her bag nervously. 'You see, I can't have children. I'd love to have a baby, but I can't.'

It took several more weeks and some very conclusive tests before Jet could be convinced that the doctor actually knew what he was talking about. And when he smilingly told her that in his experience miracles were not all that uncommon, and he saw no reason to doubt that she would produce a healthy baby in the spring, Jet was so overcome with emotion that she burst into tears on his desk.

'It's all right. It won't be that bad, my dear. I thought you *wanted* a baby.' The doctor was plainly out of his depth.

'Oh, I do, I do.' Jet lifted her face to smile at him through her tears. They were streaming down her face and her eyes were bright, watery stars as she told him in a choked, ecstatic voice that he had just made her the happiest woman in the world.

And she *was* happy. Because the baby would be Seth's. She was still happy when, much later, she began to consider the complications. Money was the main one, but she would manage somehow. Her spring exams were another, but with luck she would just have them written before the baby was born.

Then—and this was the biggest question mark of all—there was Seth. Should she tell him? He wanted children, and knowing his stern sense of responsibility he would probably want to know. But perhaps he was already married to Marian—or the other blonde. She could find out, of course. But each time she picked up the phone to call him she found she was afraid of what he might tell her, and ended up replacing the receiver on the hook. Even if he was free, did she want to trap him with the obligation of a child when he really didn't want that child's mother?

In the end Jet did nothing, and the days drifted by as she attended lectures, studied, and sometimes went out with Lara and her friends—who all said she was crazy not to get in touch with the baby's father.

Maybe she was. But she couldn't seem to do anything about it.

*   *   *

December came, and the streets were as crowded with people as the shops were with glitter and tempting displays of goods Jet couldn't afford.

On a damp, foggy evening after an unsuccessful trip to find nice but inexpensive gifts for her uncle and aunt, she pulled herself slowly up the stairs to her apartment. She was carrying a cumbersome pile of books beneath her arm and she pushed open the door thankfully, dumped them on the table by the window and sank down heavily on to one of her wooden chairs. Jet smiled to herself. She was beginning to put on weight now, although it still wasn't obvious unless she stood up.

Pulling the nearest book towards her, she picked up a pencil and started to draft out an essay on *Hamlet*.

She was so absorbed in her task that at first she didn't hear the light knock on her door. When it came again, more insistently, she lifted her hand and called irritably, 'Lara? Is that you? The door's open, why don't you just come in?' She bent her head over her books again, wishing she could convince kind-hearted Lara, who had a job and didn't have to study, that she needed to be left alone with her books in the evenings.

She was still writing furiously when it came to her, very gradually, that although the door had opened it wasn't Lara who stood at the opposite side of the table. Lara could never keep still, and this intruder was motionless as a rock.

Jet put down her pencil. Lara didn't have strong, square-tipped fingers, either—fingers which curled almost menacingly round the back of the other chair.

Jet's heart turned a great somersault, and she gave a gasp that was almost a moan as she raised her eyes slowly, painfully slowly, to the face she knew for certain she would see.

'Hello, Seth,' she whispered, after a long period of silence during which she fought to get the words past her suddenly frozen lips.

He stared at her, and his brown eyes were harder and colder than she had ever believed brown could be. 'Is that all you can say? "Hello, Seth." After putting me through almost five months of hell?'

'Hell? I don't...'

'Yes, hell.' His voice was as bleak and harsh as wind on a mountaintop. 'How did you expect me to feel when I went back to the Empress to pick you up and found only a piece of paper?'

Jet gazed up at him, feeling the colour drain from her face. And she saw that his face too was paler than usual, and thinner, although somehow that only added to his appeal. And the appeal was as strong as ever. More than anything she wanted to jump up and pull him into her arms. Not that she was much good at jumping at the moment. But she couldn't have moved anyway, because this austere, forbidding stranger was a man she didn't know.

'A piece of paper?' she finally repeated dully.

'You left me a note. Remember?'

'Oh. Yes. And it explained...'

'It explained *nothing*!' he exploded. 'It told me that since you didn't think we had much to talk about after all, you had decided to go back to Vancouver on your own. You also, if I remember rightly, thanked me for a *lovely weekend*.' He pronounced the last words with a bitter, sneering contempt.

Jet put her hands over her face so she couldn't see his hostile, accusing eyes. 'I didn't know—I thought...' she stammered through her fingers.

'*What* did you think?'

Jet swallowed, remembering how all these months she had longed to hear his voice again. Now she was hearing it, and she wished he would just go away and leave her alone to lick her wounds in peace. Then somewhere deep inside her a small spark ignited and she felt the colour returning to her cheeks as the spirit which had always kept her going fought its way back to life.

'I thought,' she said quietly, looking him straight in the eye, 'that you regretted what had happened between us. That you still hoped to marry Marian. And I didn't want you to feel you owed me anything, that you had to—let me down gently. You see, I'd already made one mistake by telling you I loved you. There was no need to make it any harder for you to escape from a situation you hadn't meant to get into. Besides...' She ran a hand wearily across her forehead. 'Besides, I didn't think I could bear to say goodbye.'

Seth stared at her for a long time as the anger slowly faded from his eyes and was replaced by confusion, distress and, finally, dismayed understanding.

'Oh, no,' he said at last, pulling out the chair he had been grasping and subsiding into it with none of his accustomed grace. There was a look in his eye as it met hers that set every nerve in her body vibrating, and she knew his need to hold her was as great as hers to be held. But he made no attempt to move towards her. Instead he reached into his pocket, made a face, and smiled wryly. 'I keep forgetting,' he explained. 'I gave up smoking when I started to look for you. At moments like these, I wish I hadn't.'

Jet smiled back uncertainly. 'You gave up smoking? I'm glad. But I don't see what I had to do with it.'

'Don't you? You see, I thought that if—no, I thought that *when* I found you, it would make you happy if I didn't smoke. Besides . . .' He shrugged. 'When I have you with me, I don't need cigarettes to relieve—stress.'

Jet eyed him suspiciously, but her glance was returned without a trace of provocation. 'I suppose not,' she agreed doubtfully. 'Although really I'm not at all sure I know what you mean.'

'Aren't you?' Now, surely, she saw the glimmerings of a grin. 'I never suspected there was anything the matter with your imagination, butterfly.'

Her heart started to thump. That grin, faint as it was, was as devastating as ever. She had to force herself to continue with quiet determination, 'Seth, if you were looking for me, if you really wanted to find me, why did you stalk in here like an avenging angel on the warpath—as if I'd committed some unforgivable crime?'

Seth leaned back in his chair and put his hands behind his head. He was wearing a dark navy pullover with a rounded neck that showed the sinews of his throat, and Jet felt the old familiar stirring of desire, followed by a small feeling of dread, because it seemed that, no matter what the future held for her, this man would always get underneath her skin, chafing and disturbing—destroying her defences. And she was afraid because although he was with her now, at any moment he might not be. But she knew she would never leave him again. Not voluntarily.

She was jolted out of her reverie when she realised Seth was replying carefully, 'First of all, I don't think angels go on the warpath. Their wings might get in the way. Secondly—oh hell, secondly I just don't know, Jet.' He brought his hands down from behind his head and rested them on the table. 'I've spent weeks searching for you. Mostly I just needed to have you with me, but sometimes I got so angry with you for disappearing that I thought if I ever found you I'd probably murder you. And that's how I felt today when I saw you sitting there writing, all calm and busy and abstracted, and not even knowing I was there.'

'I can understand that.' Jet smiled slightly. 'But what I don't understand is...'

'How I found you?'

'Well, yes, that too.' It hadn't been what she was going to ask at all. She had two much more pressing concerns than Seth's sleuthing abilities, and both of them were blonde.

But Seth, his forehead creased with the need to make sure she understood, was continuing with his own train of thought. 'When I first read your note,' he told her, 'my immediate urge was to follow you to wherever you'd gone to and murder you on the spot...'

'I wish you'd stop harping on that.'

'Shut up. I'm trying to explain. As I said, my first urge was to do you in most foully. But I couldn't, because I found I had to stay on in Victoria another day. There was trouble with the lease on our new premises, plus trouble with the new manager I'd hired. I decided to get all that

straightened out, come back on the Tuesday night—
and murder you on Wednesday.' His lips twisted.
'But as you're obviously aware, when I went round
to your place on Wednesday evening, my heartless
victim had flown. And your obnoxious friend John
took great pleasure in informing me that he had no
idea where you'd gone.' The hands which lay in
front of him on the table clenched suddenly. 'Have
you any idea what that did to me, Jet?'

Jet shook her head. 'No. No, I haven't.' Then
she smiled ruefully. 'But apparently it saved me
from your homicidal urges.' When he didn't answer,
after a while she went on hesitantly, 'Seth, I saw
that—young woman you were with outside your
office.' Her voice was very low, and the statement
was really a question.

Seth frowned. 'Young woman? What are you
talking... Oh!' His brow cleared. 'You mean
Michelle, my new assistant.'

'Is that what she is? You seemed very intimate.'

'Were you spying on me?' He sounded more
amazed than angry. Then his fist thudded down on
to the table, making her jump. 'So it *was* you I saw
across the street.' He gave a short, mirthless laugh.
'Do you realise I ran after you that morning? But
you'd already gone when I got to where I thought
I'd seen you. Of course, I didn't know that you
were only snooping.'

'I *wasn't* snooping,' exclaimed Jet hotly. 'I decided I should talk to you before I made any decision. And you were draped all over that sexy
woman. So I left.'

Seth glared at her. 'Sexy? Michelle? Are you out
of your mind? She's married to a very large football
player and she has two fairly revolting children. Her

car broke down that morning and I agreed to give her a lift. Believe me, Michelle is my assistant and that's *all*, you idiotic little...' He paused, leaned towards her and with an effort started again. 'Michelle is my assistant. I was *not* draped all over her. I was probably trying to be heard above the traffic.' His hand hit the table again. But before she could answer him the door in front of her was thrown open and a short, stocky redhead bounded into the room.

'Jet? What the hell's all the racket? Are you all...? Oh.' The redhead's eyes took in Seth's broad shoulders and his jaw jutting aggressively at Jet. 'Oh. Sorry. Am I interrupting?'

'No more than usual,' said Jet, smiling weakly. 'Lara, this is Seth.'

'Oh. Terrific. You mean this is the man...?'

'*No,*' Jet interrupted frantically. 'No, Lara, please. Not yet.'

Lara's bright gaze went from Jet's anguished dark eyes to Seth's curious ones as he twisted in his chair to stare at the newcomer. Then she shrugged. 'OK. Sorry. See you later, people.' She bounded out again, slamming the door behind her.

Seth winced. 'She's a fine one to complain about racket. What was all that about?'

'Oh, nothing. That's just Lara,' Jet murmured evasively.

'Hmm.' Seth grunted, but he didn't press the matter. 'All right. Back to Michelle. Are you satisfied now that I'm not enjoying someone else's wife and mother on the side?'

There was a bitterness in his voice which made Jet say quickly, 'Yes, of course. I'm sorry. It's just that I was so distraught at the time that I couldn't even think straight.' She saw his face soften and hastily changed the subject. 'Seth, you were telling me about how you caught up with me.'

'So I was.' He thumbed casually through one of Jet's textbooks, staring unseeing at the printed pages. 'You see, when John—and later Daisy—both assured me they didn't know where you were, I assumed you were upset for some reason about our...'

'One-night stand?'

He glanced up sharply. 'Is *that* all you thought it was?'

'No. No, of course not. I was joking.'

'Well, don't. I don't find it amusing.'

'You wouldn't,' replied Jet crossly.

Seth sighed. 'Are we going to start that again, Kellaway?'

'No. sorry. Go on.' Jet looked away from him through the window and stared at the yellow moon rising above the sea.

He gazed at her starkly. 'As I said, I knew you were upset. I decided to leave you to work it out by yourself because I was sure that, if you wanted to see me, sooner or later you would get in touch. So I waited four months.' He shut his eyes and ran his hand absently through his hair. 'Those were long months, Jet. In the end, I couldn't stand it any more. One of my clients runs a detective agency, so I hired him. It didn't take him long to find out where you were.' He gave her a crooked smile. 'So like it or not, my love, here I am.'

'Oh, Seth.' Jet saw the lines of suffering on his face, and she felt guilty and foolish and afraid and hopeful all at once. 'Oh, Scth, I'm so sorry. I didn't know—I thought you didn't—all these months I've been so unhappy.'

Seth hadn't been happy either, but there were tears running silently down her cheeks now and it occurred to him that it was the first time he had ever seen Jet cry. He reached across the small table to touch her hand. 'I'm sorry too, butterfly. I'd no idea... When I left you in the hotel that morning I didn't stop to think how things might look to you. I was late, I was confused too—and I didn't want to talk about it right then. I wanted time to think, to sort things out for myself.'

Jet nodded mistily. He had called her 'butterfly' again, and for once the word was music to her ears. Hope stirred, and blossomed in her smile.

'Seth,' she said slowly, 'I knew you were confused. But we'd been so happy. What was it you needed to think about that morning?'

His hand still covered hers and he smiled back at her, that wonderful, sexy, melting smile she had thought she would never see again. 'I needed to think about us. About the future. I needed to know if what I felt was just guilt, or something much deeper.'

'Guilt?'

He nodded. 'Yes. Guilt that I'd broken my promise to you. I still wasn't sure if I was experiencing a basically primitive urge to possess the most beautiful woman I'd ever known—or whether there was more to it than a purely physical hunger. Much more.' He turned away from her and he too stared at the moon. 'If it was just a physical need, then I knew I was going to hurt you. That's where the guilt came in again. Jet, you've no idea what it did to me, seeing you sitting there on the bed, all soft and glowing with the sweetness of morning...'

'I wasn't glowing, I was shivering.'

'Because you had no clothes on. And have you any idea what *that* did to me? I wanted to tear all my own clothes off again and tumble you back into bed. As it was, I didn't dare touch you. I'd broken a promise once, but I had no right to take from you again—to hurt you more deeply than ever.'

Still not looking at her, he waited for an answer, but when she said nothing his fingers tightened over hers and he went on slowly, 'But some time between leaving you in the hotel room and coming back to find you'd gone, I knew that I would never hurt you. There's been too much hurt in your life already. Just the thought of it made me want to hit someone, and when I realised there was no one around to hit except myself, I found out something else.' He drew his eyes slowly down from the moon until once more they were locked into hers, scorching her with their intensity. 'I learned that all I wanted was to love you, to look after you— to laugh with you. To spend the rest of my life with you, Jet.' He hesitated and then said quietly, 'Ever since Lisa, and since my mother finally left, I've vowed that when I married, my wife would be dignified, organised, practical and cool. Everything you're not, my darling.' He gave her a half-mocking smile. 'But of course, in my arrogance I hadn't allowed myself to consider that that dignified, practical breeder of sensible Hagans might also be astonishly dull.' He smiled again, and it was the tenderest, gentlest and most gloriously seductive smile she had ever seen in her life. 'Thank you for opening my eyes, butterfly—to the things that really matter. To love and laughter and...' His lips curled up wickedly at the corners. 'Other more stimulating delights.'

'Mm,' murmured Jet, turning with difficulty from the hypnotic hold of his eyes to stare primly at a point above his head. 'I suppose you mean the stimulation of your taste-buds, after years of smothering them in tobacco.'

Seth laughed. 'Witch. You know I meant nothing of the sort.' His thumb stroked her skin softly as his hand circled slowly up her arm to catch her around the elbow. Then the eyes which had been filled with laughter grew serious, and his voice was rough with emotion as, with surprising awkwardness for such a confident man, he spoke the words Jet had never thought to hear.

'I love you, butterfly. Will you marry me?'

For a moment she felt dizzy as happiness surged through her veins and joy beat a drum roll in her chest. Then, hateful and unwanted, the ugliness of reality intruded, and she knew she must not give in yet—to him or to herself. Not while the spectre of another love still lingered over their heads.

'Marian.' She spoke curtly, because she could scarcely bear to say the name.

'Marian?' Seth looked at her as if he'd never heard of his fiancée. 'Marian? I ask you to marry me and you say *Marian*?' His fingers tightened unconsciously round her elbow. 'Have you gone crazier than usual, Kellaway?'

'If you don't mind, Hagan, I find it convenient to have blood circulating in that arm. And no, I haven't gone crazy. Marian was—is?—the woman you were going to marry. Remember?'

'Ah.' Seth released her arm and stood up, the knuckles of his hands pressing hard against the table. 'No, she's not, as a matter of fact. When our two-month separation was up we decided to make the break permanent. It was a mutually agreeable decision.' He grinned, a little ruefully. 'Last time I heard, she was promoting a corpulent but financially solid stockbroker who wouldn't dream of hiring a girl in a red flowered skirt. Now, will you please answer my question?'

'Question?'

Seth gritted his teeth. 'Will you marry me, Jet Kellaway? And if you don't answer yes this time, I shall *definitely* murder you most bloodily on the spot.'

Jet laughed, and when she lifted her face to his as he stood over her, it was radiant and glowing with love. 'It sounds as though I don't have much choice, doesn't it? Yes, of course I'll marry you, Seth, darling. I...'

But Seth didn't let her finish. In a flash he was round the table, and seizing both her hands in his.

'Seth, there is just one thing,' she murmured quickly, resisting his efforts to pull her to her feet.

'Like hell there is. I've waited five months, Jet, and I'm not waiting any longer.'

'Yes, but...'

'No buts.' His fingers closed over her shoulders and he pulled her forcefully out of her chair.

'Wait, Seth. Please. There's something I have to tell you.'

'No. There's nothing you have to tell me. Not now.' Now she was standing close in front of him, so close that he could only see her face. His arms moved around what was left of her waist and his lips covered hers demandingly and possessed them in a long, breathtaking kiss.

Jet's eyes were closed and her hands were already exploring the smooth tough skin beneath his sweater, when she felt his body stiffen and pull back.

Slowly, very slowly, he detached her arms from behind his neck and held her away from him, his eyes travelling deliberately over her loose red smock to the noticeably distended figure below the waist. And as he stared, at first in total disbelief, she saw his greenish-brown eyes turn almost amber as they lit with a flame that to her horrified gaze seemed nothing nothing short of volcanic. He was angry. Incredibly angry.

But the eruption when it came was very quiet.

'You didn't tell me. It's been almost five months, Jet, and you didn't tell me.' His voice was flat, and curiously without inflection.

'I didn't know for a long time,' she explained desperately. 'I didn't believe it was true.'

'No. And when you did know?' His tone was still blank, expressing nothing.

'I—I didn't know what to do... I wanted to phone you...'

'But you didn't.'

'No...'

'Hell, Jet.' His face was very near to hers and the cleft in his chin seemed carved like the mark of a knife. But the fire in his eyes had gone out, and with an exclamation which Jet could not interpret he struck his hand savagely against the table, spun on his heel and strode swiftly out of the room.

As the door crashed closed behind him, Jet cried his name in a wail that would have raised the rafters if there had been any. As it was, in no time at all it had raised Lara, who streaked through the still vibrating door like a bloodhound on the trail of a hare.

But it was no hare that met the redhead's anxious gaze. Only Jet's lovely eyes, dark with sorrow, and a face glazed with such unbearable anguish that Lara felt a frightening jab of fear.

CHAPTER ELEVEN

'WHAT'S happened? Are you OK, Jet?' Lara's eyes were wide with alarm as she took in her friend's wild, distraught stare and the way her hands were scrabbling at the edge of the table for support.

Jet turned to face her, and her normally golden complexion was streaked with blotches of red. 'It's Seth,' she whispered. 'He asked me to marry him...'

'But that's wonderful.'

'No, it's terrible. I was sitting down. He didn't know about the baby, and when he saw...' She turned away and her long dark hair fell across her face in a curtain that hid her eyes. But Lara had seen her stumble, and in an instant she was at Jet's side and helping her into the room's one over-stuffed chair.

'Here. You sit down. Take it easy. Now...' She perched herself on the table, flattening Jet's favourite history text in the process. 'Now, tell Aunt Lara what's the matter.'

Jet sniffed and dug into her pocket for a handkerchief, although she showed no signs of giving way to tears. 'He's gone,' she said bleakly. 'Seth's gone. And I don't suppose he'll ever come back.'

'Because you're having a baby?'

'I don't think so. I think it's because I didn't let him know.'

'What did I tell you? What did we *all* tell you?' Lara began to crow. Then, seeing Jet's stricken face, she said quickly, 'I'm sorry. "I-told-you-so"s don't help much, do they? What you need is a good stiff brandy. Do you have any?'

'Of course not. Anyway, it's bad for the baby.'

'All right, coffee, then. You've got to have something.' Lara disappeared into the tiny kitchen, and Jet heard her banging cups about on the counter. A few minutes later she was back with two cups of steaming coffee.

Jet took one, put it down on the floor beside her and stared at Lara with eyes that seemed to see nothing. Wide, vacant eyes that made Lara a little afraid.

'Don't, Jet,' she said kindly. 'Don't let that skunk hurt you any more.'

'Skunk? He's not a skunk. And I think this time I'm the one who's hurt him.' Jet's voice was so low and sad that Lara could barely hear her.

'He's a skunk,' she repeated firmly.

And Jet didn't care enough to argue. What did it matter what Lara called him? She sat gazing through the window at the moon, and all she could think of was that happiness for her seemed as elusive and unattainable as the golden crescent hanging in the sky. It had been so close. For a moment she had almost held it. But Seth had carried hope away with him forever when he'd disappeared through that door, and this time it was harder to bear than ever. If he had stayed away, never asked her to marry him, then she had already proved she could learn to live with that. But now? Could she start all over, pull herself together yet again and try to make a life for herself and Seth's child? She didn't know any more. Just at the moment all of her feelings seemed frozen. Without

Seth, there was a void in the place where her heart should be and his reappearance had only deepened it, made it darker...

The minutes ticked by and the moon grew brighter. Lara sat quietly, watching her friend, not wanting to leave her alone. Eventually, when she couldn't stand the inactivity any longer, she went into the kitchen to make more coffee. She had to do *something* to stir Jet from this seemingly desperate lethargy.

When she came back, Jet was no longer looking at the moon but at the door. Not as if it meant anything, but rather as a prisoner, for want of anything else to do, might study a fly on the wall.

Lara followed the direction of her eyes. Then she blinked. Surely she was seeing things? No. She wasn't. The handle was definitely turning. Very slowly, but turning none the less. She glanced at her watch. It had been a long three hours since that skunk had walked out on poor Jet. He couldn't possibly be coming back now.

'Do you have a poker anywhere about?' she whispered.

'No.' Jet shook her head, not minding much what danger might lurk in the corridor outside. But she could see that Lara minded. 'There's a knife in the kitchen, if you like,' she suggested listlessly.

Lara nodded. The door was inching open. Hastily she grabbed two knives from the counter and handed the smaller one to Jet, who accepted it without even looking at her.

Then, as whoever was behind the door swung it wide, Lara leaped across the room. Swirling the knife about her head like a cutlass, she let out a blood-curdling yell.

The man who had just entered stopped dead, then with a startled exclamation he ducked gracefully under the wildly flailing weapon before whipping round to grab Lara by the wrist.

'I'll take that, Captain Blood,' he said firmly, twisting the knife deftly out of her grasp.

Lara gaped at him. 'Heavens, it is the skunk, after all!' she gasped.

'At your service,' said Seth drily. Then he turned to where Jet was still rooted in her chair. 'Oh, no. Not another pirate,' he murmured, moving quickly to her side to remove the small blade which was pointing directly at his abdomen.

She didn't move. 'Jet?' he said softly. There was no answer. He tried again. 'Butterfly?'

At that, she did look up. 'Hello, Seth,' she whispered, in a voice he could hardly hear.

Seth closed his eyes. 'Isn't this where I came in?'

There was a movement behind him, but when he turned round it was only to see a mop of red hair vanishing through a door which for the first time that evening was being closed with a considerate lack of noise.

Seth took both Jet's hands in his. They were very cold. He sat down on the wide arm of her chair and his right thigh brushed against her knee. He saw that her eyes had turned from him again and she was staring down at the floor.

'Jet,' he asked gently, not wanting to distress the fragile figure beside him, 'Jet, why all the weaponry?'

'I don't know,' replied Jet wearily. 'I think Lara thought you were a rapist.'

The ghost of a smile flickered across his lips. 'Not in your condition, sweetheart. I only rape ladies who aren't quite so obviously spoken for.' Lightly his fingers touched the swelling below her waist.

When she heard the soft, caressing note in his voice Jet lifted her head. Was this the same man who had stalked out three hours ago in a flaming temper? She looked into his eyes and knew it was, but there was no anger in them now, only a bright, consuming tenderness—and a very gentle passion.

She smiled tremulously. When his hands tightened over hers, she added hesitantly, 'I know why you went away, Seth, but—why did you come back, like a rapist in the night?' Her smile was firmer now and the laughter even reached her eyes.

'I came back because I couldn't do anything else—didn't *want* to do anything else.' He smiled wryly. 'But I didn't mean to pose as your friendly neighbourhood rapist. It's after midnight, you know. I thought you might be asleep, so I decided just to try the door quietly. When I saw your light was on, I pushed it open.' He grinned. 'Only to be confronted by a redheaded assault-force with all knives blazing—and a dark-haired zombie with a particularly murderous eye.'

Jet giggled. It was a doubtful sort of giggle, but still definitely a giggle. 'It wasn't murderous. I just—didn't believe it was you.'

The amusement in Seth's eyes faded and his hands moved up to her shoulders. 'I'm sorry, but-terfly,' he murmured with deep sincerity. His head bent towards her mouth. 'Can you ever forgive me?'

'There's nothing to forgive, Seth. I love you.'

'And I love you.'

It was a very long time later that Seth disen-tangled his legs from hers and her fingers from his hair, to remark plaintively that he really didn't think there was room enough for the three of them in the chair. 'I'll never be the same again,' he grumbled. 'My body feels like a twisted tree-trunk.'

'Well, it doesn't look like one,' Jet teased him as he stood up. 'I've never had the least desire to go to bed with a tree.'

At that, Seth gave a shout of laughter and bent down to scoop her out of the chair. 'Now that you mention it,' he murmured, 'I think bed's a very good idea. For you. You look all in.'

With one arm under her knees and the other beneath her shoulders, he took two steps across the room, staggered, and put her down.

'Remind me not to carry you across the threshold,' he muttered. 'I'd forgotten you're eating for two.'

'As a matter of fact, I am,' she said smugly. 'You should be pleased. You always were trying to fatten me for Christmas.'

'So I was,' he agreed, putting an arm around her waist and leading her to the open door of her small bedroom. 'Come on, little turkey. Time to sleep.'

But Jet hung back. 'Seth, we still have to talk.'

'I know we do,' he said quietly, smiling into her eyes. 'In the morning.'

Jet nodded, satisfied. 'Yes,' she acceded happily. 'In the morning I'll be able to think straight. Just now I don't really want to.'

It was almost afternoon before either of them was in the mood for thinking, and by that time they had slept quietly in each other's arms for hours.

Seth slipped his long, bare legs out of bed, and Jet watched him as he loped out into the kitchen clad only in a pale orange blanket. She smiled, a long, curving, sensuous smile, and lay back on the pillows with a soft, contented sigh.

A few minutes later Seth was back bearing coffee. When he reached the side of the bed he paused, a look of startled consternation on his face.

'You *can* drink coffee, can't you?' he asked anxiously. 'Doesn't it sometimes make pregnant ladies—ill?'

'Sometimes, but I'm past that stage now. So you can wait on me all you like.'

He grinned. 'Not a chance. And if you don't wait on me satisfactorily, I shall turn to Mrs Crabtree.'

'Mrs Crabtree? Ah, yes, but Mrs Crabtree won't provide the kind of service I've noticed you seem to require.' Jet stuck her tongue out at him.

'Poisonous butterfly,' chuckled Seth. Then his eyes became serious as he added quietly, 'We still have to talk, don't we, sweetheart?'

'Yes,' she agreed, running a languid hand down his thigh as he perched on the edge of the bed.

He moved away from her. 'But we never will if you keep on doing that.'

She sighed. 'No. You're right. Seth?'

'Mm?'

'Have you really forgiven me for not telling you about the baby?'

He nodded. 'Of course I have. At first I was so stunned and angry, I couldn't even talk to you. You see, it was an incredible shock...'

'Yes. I'm sorry,' she whispered.

He shook his head. 'No, it's not your fault. It wasn't that I didn't want the baby, it was just that— I'd come to terms with the fact that you couldn't have children, and in the end it didn't even matter. Without you, my life would have been so empty and alone that children just didn't seem very important any more. But if I'd known ... Jet, I'm not the sort of man who goes around littering the world with children who never know their own father. When I saw how it was with you, I was shocked, hurt and angry—but mostly I was ashamed. Ashamed that you had had to bear everything on your own, but hurt and angry too because you hadn't given me the chance to share the burden.' Absently he leaned forward to smooth her hair back from her eyes. 'I do understand why. I know you were confused and hurt too. But at that moment I had to get away, I had to get out in the air just to be by myself. To think.'

'And it only took you three hours.'

'Was it three hours?' He picked up her hand and began to trace the lines across her palm. 'It seemed longer. I don't even know where I went. But of course, in the end I knew there was only one thing I could do. I think I'd known that all along. So I came back. And I'm so very sorry I made you unhappy again.'

Jet smiled, a languorous smile laced with mischief. 'I was unhappy, but I'm not unhappy any longer.' Her smile broadened. 'Besides, Lara did help me to get some of my own back, didn't she? She almost stabbed you with the breadknife.'

Seth raised his eyebrows and shuddered. 'You mean the redheaded battleaxe? Is she always like that?'

'Mostly.'

'In that case, I'm glad we'll be living in Vancouver.'

'Oh!' exclaimed Jet, surprised. 'Yes, I suppose we will. But ...'

'But what?'

'But I'm going to university *here*. Your detective must have told you that.'

Seth nodded. 'He did. Do you want to finish your year?'

Jet stared ahead of her, but her mind was shifting back over the years to a past which was filled with failure and things started but left undone.

'Yes,' she said finally. 'Yes, Seth, this time I think I must.'

'I'm glad. Not glad we'll have to be apart sometimes, but glad you're doing what you want. Besides, we can spend weekends together, and it will only be for a few months. Next year you can transfer to one of the Vancouver universities.' He grinned. 'Meanwhile, I think I'm going to find that the new branch of Hagan's in Victoria will take up a great deal of my time.'

'University in Vancouver?' Jet looked startled. 'You know, I honestly hadn't thought past the end of this year. Not since I knew about the baby. But I could, couldn't I? Transfer, I mean.'

'If you want to.'

'I'm not sure,' Jet mused. 'Sooner or later I *know* I'll get my degree, I'm certain of that now. But—the baby...'

'Why not play it by ear, then? Make the decision when the time comes.'

'Yes.' Jet nodded. 'Yes, I think that *is* what I'd like to do.'

'And meanwhile we'll be married in three days' time. I've already got the licence, and my father, who is utterly delighted, has promised to book the church.'

'At this short notice? He can't possibly.'

'Oh, yes, he can. You don't know my father.'

'Huh. Very sure of yourselves, the two of you, weren't you?' she teased, leaning forward to place her hand provocatively back on his thigh.

'No. Just hoping. With you around, I'll never be sure of anything.' He pushed her gently back against the pillows and leaned up on one elbow beside her.

'Uncertainty is good for you. Keeps you on your toes,' she retorted.

'Not likely. In this case it's keeping me in your bed.'

'So it is.' Jet's eyes were sparkling with laughter as she wrapped her arms around his neck and pulled his head down next to hers.

'Do you think we should have a boy or a girl?' she asked dreamily some time later, as they lingered over baked beans on toast.

'A girl. With big, dark eyes just like her mother's.'

Jet shook her head. 'You'd spoil her dreadfully. I think we'd better have a boy just like you.'

Four months after their wedding Jet confidently wrote her exams. And, just two days after that, both of their wishes were granted when she gave birth to healthy twins.

The next day Seth, whose face still showed signs of the strain of a sleepless night, sank down in the chair beside Jet's bed and groaned. 'Twins!' he exploded. 'Twins! Who would have thought it?' And then as the implications of this double jeopardy sank in with all its unnerving possibilities, 'Help.'

Jet smiled tenderly into her husband's face, which expressed love and pride and consternation in almost equal measures. 'I know,' she agreed understandingly. 'It is a bit intimidating, isn't it? All that washing.'

'Washing? Oh, Mrs Crabtree will see to that. It's all that howling I'm concerned about.'

'Howling?'

'Hm. Babies howl, don't they?'

'No. Wolves do. Babies cry.'

'Hmm,' murmured Seth doubtfully. 'I suppose that will make all the difference.'

His tone was so lugubrious that it made Jet burst out laughing. 'Don't worry,' she consoled him impishly, as she trailed her fingers gently down his cheek. 'I'm sure Sebastian and Susannah will never want to cry.'

'Sebastian and Susannah? Oh, no.' He pulled her hand from his face and regarded her with mock horror. 'We're not calling them anything so frivolous. They'll have nice sensible names—like James and Janet.'

Jet sighed dolefully. 'And I thought I'd cured you of being sensible,' she teased.

'There are limits, butterfly. James and Janet. And that settles it.'

It didn't, though, and eight weeks later, at their grandfather's insistence, two lusty babies were christened Seth and Jetta. He said it was the only way they would ever have names at all.

'And very good names, too,' he asserted, in a voice which brooked no discussion. 'They've done perfectly well for you two, and you can't argue about *that*.'

'No, we can't,' agreed Seth, his eyes bright with pride and devilment. 'And now that we've called my daughter Jetta, to avoid confusion there's only one possible name left for her mother.'

'Yes. Jet,' said the owner of that name with conviction.

Seth shook his head. 'Not a chance, love. You've always been "butterfly" to me. And now you'll be my butterfly forever.'

HARLEQUIN
Romance

Coming Next Month

#3061 ONE MORE SECRET Katherine Arthur
Writing detective stories as Joe Rocco was Kelsey's secret life, but could she keep it secret when Bart Malone appealed for Joe's help in a real mystery? Bart seemed hard to resist—but was there more than one mystery?

#3062 DANCING SKY Bethany Campbell
When Adam MacLaren, with his chain of modern discount stores, invades Dancing Sky, no one is safe. Not Mitzi's fiancé or the rest of the retailers. And least of all Mitzi. She finds herself singled out for the greatest upheaval of all.

#3063 PASSION'S FAR SHORE Madeleine Ker
Dorothy had accepted the job as governess to Pearl, not because she wanted to go to Japan, but because the little girl really needed her. But it seemed that Pearl's father, Calum Hescott, thought differently....

#3064 NO ACCOUNTING FOR LOVE Eva Rutland
Clay Kencade is a risk-taker. He's got a knack for business and a way with women. So why has he fallen for serious, reserved Cindy Rogers, who's as cautious in her personal life as she is in business?

#3065 FROZEN ENCHANTMENT Jessica Steele
Jolene was delighted at the unexpected offer of traveling to Russia with the boss of Templeton's as his temporary secretary. But she soon discovered it was not going to be such fun, for Cheyne Templeton had already made up his mind what kind of girl Jolene was....

#3066 MASTER OF CASHEL Sara Wood
Caitlin resented Jake Ferriter for taking her beloved home, Cashelkerry, and blamed him for causing her father's death. But she could not deny the attraction she felt for this enigmatic, ruthless man. The feeling was mutual—but could she cope with his offer of an affair without commitment....

Available in June wherever paperback books are sold, or through Harlequin Reader Service:

In the U.S.
901 Fuhrmann Blvd.
P.O. Box 1397
Buffalo, N.Y. 14240-1397

In Canada
P.O. Box 603
Fort Erie, Ontario
L2A 5X3

Harlequin Regency Romance™

Romance the way it was *always* meant to be!

The time is 1811, when a Regent Prince rules the empire. The place is London, the glittering capital where rakish dukes and dazzling debutantes scheme and flirt in a dangerously exciting game. Where marriage is the passport to wealth and power, yet every girl hopes secretly for love....

Welcome to Harlequin Regency Romance where reading is an adventure and romance is *not* just a thing of the past! Two delightful books a month.

Available wherever Harlequin Books are sold.

Have You Ever Wondered If You Could Write A Harlequin Novel?

Here's great news—Harlequin is offering a series of cassette tapes to help you do just that. Written by Harlequin editors, these tapes give practical advice on how to make your characters—and your story—come alive. There's a tape for each contemporary romance series Harlequin publishes.

Mail order only

All sales final

HARLEQUIN
American Romance

THE LOVES OF A CENTURY...

Join American Romance in a nostalgic look back at the Twentieth Century—at the lives and loves of American men and women from the turn-of-the-century to the dawn of the year 2000.

Journey through the decades from the dance halls of the 1900s to the discos of the seventies ... from Glenn Miller to the Beatles ... from Valentino to Newman ... from corset to miniskirt ... from beau to Significant Other.

Relive the moments ... recapture the memories.

Look now for the CENTURY OF AMERICAN ROMANCE series in Harlequin American Romance. In one of the four American Romance titles appearing each month, for the next twelve months, we'll take you back to a decade of the Twentieth Century, where you'll relive the years and rekindle the romance of days gone by.

Don't miss a day of the CENTURY OF AMERICAN ROMANCE.

A CENTURY OF
AMERICAN ROMANCE
1900's

The women...the men...the passions...
the memories....

CAR-1